**WATERMARKED**

The body of the dead woman has been in the Severn for some time, drifting downstream, and it is not a pleasant sight.

The river has washed away much of the forensic evidence. There is enough there, however, to suggest to Superintendent Lambert and Detective Sergeant Bert Hook that she did not meet her death by accident.

Slowly and patiently they build up a picture of a woman of contradictions: a woman who harboured secret passions. But time is running out, for the killer is watching them and is ready to strike again . . .

**BY THE SAME AUTHOR**

STRANGLEHOLD
THE FOX IN THE FOREST
DEAD ON COURSE
BRING FORTH YOUR DEAD
FOR SALE – WITH CORPSE
MURDER AT THE NINETEENTH

# WATERMARKED

J. M. Gregson

Collins Crime
An imprint of HarperCollins*Publishers*
77–85 Fulham Palace Road, London W6 8JB

First published in Great Britain
in 1994 by Collins Crime

1 3 5 7 9 8 6 4 2

© J. M. Gregson 1994

J. M. Gregson asserts the moral right to be
identified as the author of this work.

A catalogue record for this book is
available from the British Library

ISBN 0 00 232498 9

Text set in Baskerville

Photoset by Rowland Phototypesetting Ltd
Bury St Edmunds, Suffolk
Printed and bound in Great Britain by
HarperCollins Book Manufacturing, Glasgow

All rights reserved. No part of this publication may be
reproduced, stored in a retrieval system, or transmitted,
in any form or by any means, electronic, mechanical,
photocopying, recording or otherwise, without the prior
permission of the publishers.

# CHAPTER ONE

The Severn is the longest river in England and Wales.

It winds for two hundred and ten miles through the historic shires of middle England. Old Father Thames may be more famous because of his metropolitan connections, but the silver Severn has some powerful admirers. Shakespeare wrote of how the river 'hid his crisp head in hollow bank' while mighty battles in the Wars of the Roses shook the ground around it and shaped the course of English history.

In its final, tidal stages, it has the phenomenon of the Severn bore, that six-foot-high wave which sweeps dramatically inward with the rise of the tide. But in the stage before this last one, the river traces a lazy, serpentine route between the ancient cathedrals of Worcester and Gloucester, sneaking a look at the great abbey of Tewkesbury on its way.

There are tracts here where the river moves very slowly, passing between rich water meadows, which are all the greener from the floods the great river visits frequently upon them. Here the water seems on warm summer days to be scarcely moving at all, and any floating matter moves very gradually upon the sluggish waters. Sometimes such debris is held for a time on the soft ground at the edge of one of the huge bends, where willows reach their low boughs far out over the water, trapping matter for a while among their exposed roots at the edge of the river.

That is what had happened to the body.

It had been in the summer water for some days. Even the farmer who found it was in no doubt of that. The torso was swollen beneath the clothes, and the pallid skin was stretched like the rubber of an obscene balloon over what was left of the features. Some furtive creature with small, fierce teeth had attacked both the face and the area of the forearm which protruded beyond the sodden dark wool of the sleeve.

The day was still and warm; even the narrow leaves of the willow, so sensitive to the slightest breeze, scarcely rustled above the water. In the dense patch of shade beneath the arching willow, it was still and dark, but beyond it where the sun blazed, the broad, still waters of the Severn made a mirror for the trees on the opposite bank, concealing the slow tug of the current beneath that smooth surface.

The farmer was a man of experience. He had seen death among his cattle, often, and he was hardened to the squeals of the abattoir. But he was not prepared for this human death, which came upon him before he had time to prepare himself for it. He had the presence of mind to turn sharply away from the corpse before he vomited.

Apart from a little movement of the sun towards the west, the essentials of the scene did not change at all from the moment the farmer's dog left the cows and drew him with his barking to the corpse at the water's edge until the time two hours later when the Scene of Crime team had marked off the surrounding area with white tapes.

The body lay with its head nearest to the shore, amid the deep scorings made in the soft red earth by the hooves of the cattle as they came to drink in the shade. One eye had gone—pecked away, no doubt, by the carrion crows that screeched raucously from the highest oak two fields away from the river. Long strands of wet hair were draped decently across the other side of the face, concealing whatever ravages might have been wrought there. There were no wrinkles because of the swelling: indeed, the white skin with its tinge of green looked scarcely human at all.

The bloated legs lay half submerged in the water; the single toe which showed above the surface had a film of what might be nylon around it. The calves were beneath the muddy water, but there was what looked like the hem of a skirt on the surface. It looked as if this thing might once have been a woman. A lady, perhaps: no harm now in allowing that.

Sergeant Johnson had seen many worse corpses than this one. He could tell at a glance that it had been dead for several days at least, but he did not waste time on speculations. He directed his Scene of Crime team calmly and efficiently as they began their assiduous search of the area. The officers knew the routine: they must miss no small clue as to the identity of this body and more importantly, how it came to be in this particular spot.

It was in some respects a formality, for Johnson was already sure in his own mind that this death had not occurred in this quiet spot. His men found nothing of particular significance, and it was not long before he gave permission for the remains to be eased into the body bag. The ambulance lurched carefully away across the field's undulations, which were baked hard by the long hours of late spring sun.

Sergeant Johnson took a last look round the scene before he left. The tapes could stay here for the moment; let some higher rank take the decisions he was paid for. But he had seen no need to leave a PC on guard over the site through the night. He trudged across the field to the lane where he had left his car. This death, despite its muted discovery, was not without interest. Drownings did not usually excite his professional attention. Of those which were not accidental, the majority were suicides.

But any injuries upon a body were always of interest until the cause of death had been established. The most nauseating marks upon this one had probably occurred during its prolonged immersion in the Severn. There was one laceration, though, upon which Johnson's keen eye had dwelt at length, even though it was whitened by the water.

It was a livid scar across the throat of the corpse.

## CHAPTER TWO

Dr Cyril Burgess was indulging in one of his favourite hobbies—the baiting of Superintendent John Lambert.

The starting point for what he saw as his harmless fun was the delicacy of the superintendent's stomach where the physical details of post-mortems were concerned. It allowed the pathologist an infinite variety of small threats, as he pretended with each new piece of information to reveal the item which had prompted his conclusions and speculations.

Burgess had kept his rubber ankle-length boots on; they carried a suggestion that he might at any moment take up the knives he had recently laid down and resume his charnel house activities. The tap beneath the dissecting table, which was used to wash away excess blood and offal, had been left running gently; Burgess noted with satisfaction how Lambert's eyes were drawn back to it at intervals, as if he expected to see new gouts of blood reddening the water as it spread silently over the stainless steel and ran to the drain.

There had, in fact, been very little blood flowing from this sadly deteriorated corpse, but Burgess saw no reason to apprise John Lambert of that fact.

'I've followed the routine procedures for violent death, in case we have to account for ourselves with some legal eagle in due course, but of course, many of them are almost meaningless with a corpse of this age.' He wrinkled his lips with distaste, making the thought sound like a rebuke to the superintendent for presenting him with such imperfect materials for his macabre work.

Lambert saw an opening and went for it, but he was not quite quick enough. 'Yes, how long would you say it is since—'

'I've weighed the heart, brain, spleen, lungs and the other

organs as usual.' He gestured towards the empty stainless steel bench next to the one where the husk of the body lay beneath its sheet. A series of dishes were laid out here. Each was at present covered with a cloth, but Burgess gave the impression that he might at any moment spring to reveal their contents, like a demented waiter demonstrating his menu to an unsuspecting customer. 'But of course, the deterioration is such that reliable deductions are scarcely possible.'

Burgess plucked at the cuffs of his pristine white coat and looked at the squares of cloth with sudden distaste, as if he thought it deceitful of him not to reveal the full paucity of the decaying organs beneath them. The scent of that decay was beginning to outweigh the liberal applications of formaldehyde which were supposed to disguise it.

Lambert said desperately, 'We've no idea as yet who it is. We're going to need all the help you can give us.'

He could have said nothing better to divert Burgess from his slaughterhouse humour. The pathologist, though most of his ideas of detection were derived from the crime fiction of an earlier age, was always anxious to be involved in the business of an investigation. When he was not being impish—and sometimes even when he was—he could be both shrewd and informative. He liked to be involved as part of the team in an investigation, and Lambert found it useful to humour that small vanity whenever he could. The two men, who both felt themselves increasingly the representatives of an earlier and simpler age, liked and respected each other's skills.

Burgess said with a businesslike air, 'She's female. Her death wasn't an accident. Nor was it suicide. And she didn't drown. She was dumped in the water after death.'

'How long after death?'

'That's impossible to say with any certainty, I'm afraid. The body has been in the river for at least a week, and certain evidence has disappeared. Now, with a body which had been in a warm house in this weather, the development of maggots in the decaying organs would have enabled us to be fairly precise about the time of death . . .' His eyes brightened wistfully at the picture the thought brought to his vivid mind.

'What else can you tell me about her?' Lambert insisted on thinking of that collection of deteriorating flesh and gristle which Burgess had spread over two tables as a human being. That would be the person he had to present to grieving relatives, when they were eventually located. That would be the person he had to discover for himself; a murder hunt always moved out from the victim. When you knew all that was possible to know about the victim and her way of life, you could begin to determine your suspects.

Burgess pursed his lips and began to organize his thoughts for delivery. He was a scientist, even before the medical man he had once been. The attraction of this job was that it afforded him the scientific certainties which living bodies never permitted to the physician. He could dismember the dead and investigate their components until he arrived at the certainties which were never possible for the living. The dead had no pride, no modesty, no pain to be considered. And they were never in a hurry.

He said, 'She was between forty and fifty. She had had children, probably more than one. It seems that she was married: she had worn a wedding ring on what is left of the third finger of her left hand.' He moved as if to lift the sheet from the table next to him, but Lambert's hastily raised arm signified that he did not need the visual demonstration.

The superintendent said, 'You say "had worn". Does that imply theft?' So straightforward a motive for murder would be something of a relief.

'Hardly. There was what looks like an expensive brooch left untouched on the woman's blouse. The ring is probably somewhere at the bottom of the Severn; something has eaten most of the finger. I can show you if you—'

'There's no need! I'll take your word.' Lambert chose not to notice the pathologist's disappointment.

A wedding ring meant that there were probably a husband and children somewhere, who did not know of this. The missing persons' register had not yet thrown up anyone who fitted the details of the corpse taken from the river. To be more accurate, no one in the family had reported the disappearance of a wife and a mother. That might be the most significant fact so far—the family were involved in some way in four-fifths of murders.

Lambert said, 'You say she did not die from drowning?' It was an oblique way of arriving at the question he wanted to ask about the real cause of death. Perhaps he feared that if he asked that question more directly the sheet might be flung back with a stage magician's triumphant flourish to reveal the handiwork beneath it.

Burgess considered whether to do just that. But he knew that the combined effects of the water, the Severn's small creatures and his own dissection were particularly horrific. Moreover, the ravages which had gone on before he began his cutting made for an untidy impression, and he abhorred untidiness in his laboratory.

Besides, it was more amusing to him to tease the superintendent than actually to shock and revolt him. He said, 'She was strangled. Some sort of ligature around the neck. She was certainly quite dead when she went into the water. My guess is that she had been dead for some hours, but probably not more than a day. When you get my written report, you will see that is an opinion based on my findings, not a fact.'

Lambert understood the distinction he was making. In court, even strongly held expert opinion would be easily discounted by a jury worked on by an expert counsel, whereas what was stated as a medical fact was usually simply accepted. He said, 'There is no possibility that she hanged herself, that someone was merely covering up a suicide?'

He was thinking of a CID division in the north of England which had spent months on a murder investigation that never was, because a churchman who still saw suicide as shameful and sinful had chosen to dump a relative who had hanged himself and simulate a murder.

'No possibility whatsoever, John.' Burgess's satisfaction was manifest. 'Death was swift in this case, and the nature of the wound does not indicate that the woman hung from a beam. There is no sign of cerebral anaemia. I should be pretty certain myself that someone took her by surprise from behind and killed her within a few seconds.'

'What kind of ligature. Rope? Piano wire?'

Burgess shook his head. 'That's where a week in the Severn has done its work, I'm afraid. Forensic have got tissue samples of the throat skin from around the wound, but I shall be very surprised if they can give you anything from them. Any fibres of rope or string have long since been washed away. The scar, or what's left of it, looks a little too wide to have been anything as thin or sharp as piano wire, but that's as far as I'd care to go.' Burgess dropped his voice into an appalling parody of a B-movie Hollywood policeman. 'It looks like you've gotten yourself a tough case to crack, Officer.'

Lambert, refusing to react, said stiffly, 'She doesn't seem to you like a derelict, does she?'

'Not from what's left of her, no. Her teeth are in good condition and have had regular attention. I'd say she was well-nourished and healthy, and probably pretty fit for her age.'

Lambert nodded. 'That tallies with the obvious things about her clothing. The underwear was the ubiquitous Marks and Spencers, but the labels in the sweater and skirt indicate good quality items, one of them from a rather exclusive shop in Worcester. We'll get the full forensic report in due course, but I expect the water will have removed everything which might have been useful.'

'I'm sure it will.' Burgess beamed his satisfaction: this

looked like an intriguing mystery, just when heart attacks and road accidents had been providing pretty dull fare for an imaginative mortician. 'But there are still one or two marks on the body which provide food for thought.'

Lambert recognized that as usual Burgess had left his most interesting information until last. He said eagerly, 'And what would those be?'

His eagerness was his undoing. It allowed Burgess to feel that a demonstration was called for, and he snatched the sheet back dramatically from the lower limbs of the corpse. Lambert saw a milk-white foot, goose-fleshed from prolonged immersion, with one of the swollen toes missing and the flesh at the heel nibbled down to the bone.

Burgess said calmly, 'That's just minor damage caused by the creatures of the Severn. I suspect a pike might have had a nibble or two, but my piscatorial knowledge is very limited. But what will interest you, John, are these marks here.' He pointed at a blackened area of flesh above the ankle with his ball pen, then moved the sheet a little to show a similar mark on the other leg, just below the calf.

Lambert forced himself to look at these significant areas, striving hard for the tunnel vision that would shut out the rest of those incomplete feet. 'These couldn't have occurred while the body was in the river?'

'Hardly. They're too regular, for one thing. And the nature of the bruising indicates that the damage was done soon after death.'

'Not before?' Lambert had sudden visions, of kidnapping and torture, of sadistic maniacs who did not need a motive to kill.

'It's difficult to be certain with a body in this state, but I don't think so. For one thing, the bruising would probably be more severe if it had occurred in life. For another, there is no evidence that the woman struggled, as she would surely have done had she been alive—unless her hands had been tied also, which they plainly weren't.'

'So how do you interpret this?'

'Oh, that's for detectives, not struggling pathologists.' Burgess was at his most irritating when being both urbane and modest.

Lambert knew his man well enough to produce the sentiments required of him. 'Come on, Cyril, speculate a little for me. No one will ask you to stand by it in court.'

Burgess was delighted. He dropped again into his appalling American accent for his first phrase. 'OK, Officer, Ah'll play a hunch. Well, it seems to me that someone was trying to weight the corpse, to hold it down on the bed of the river. I think a weight of some kind was attached to the ankles of this woman by rope or string. Perhaps it was hurriedly or carelessly attached; perhaps some creature of the river helped to remove it. Perhaps the person who attached the weight even intended that the corpse should be free to float to the surface after a few days, but that seems over-subtle.'

'I agree. The likeliest explanation is that whoever weighted the body intended that it would remain undiscovered, either permanently or for a long period. He or she must have had a reason for that. Of course, anything which makes us uncertain about the precise time of a death immediately makes an investigation difficult.'

To Lambert's relief, they now moved back into the small, neat office where Burgess kept his records and his reference books. They had hardly arrived there when the phone rang. Burgess gave his name, then passed the phone to Lambert. 'It's your Inspector Rushton from the Murder Room,' he said, rolling the last phrase off his tongue with relish.

Lambert knew from Rushton's slightly self-important tone that he had some news. The voice on the other end of the line said, 'I think we have an identification for the victim, sir.'

## CHAPTER THREE

In the end, the day turned out to be rather an anticlimax for Ivy Evans.

Mrs Evans was the cleaning lady at The Beeches, though she preferred to describe herself as 'Mrs Pritchard's domestic' when she answered the phone. She did not need to do that very often, for she went to the house only once a week—on Tuesday mornings. Mrs Pritchard would have preferred her to go on Fridays, to get the house spruce for the weekend, but she had explained that her regulars—by which she meant the people who employed her for two days each week—had priority on that day. Mrs Pritchard had accepted the Tuesdays which were all that she could offer meekly enough when she explained. Mrs Evans concluded that that meant that she was a good cleaner.

In truth, The Beeches was an easy house to clean: there were only two adults in occupation, and no small children to worry about. Mrs Evans liked children, but they made work in a house, there was no doubt about that. Her other two employers had four children and three dogs between them, and there was much more work in their houses than in The Beeches. Besides, there wasn't the satisfaction in cleaning when you knew the place was going to be as untidy as ever within a few hours. She had come to look forward to returning to the peaceful serenity of the gracious rooms and fitted carpets of The Beeches.

On this June morning, it had seemed a particularly attractive prospect as she walked out from the village to the big house at its edge. The hawthorn was fresh and scented in the hedges; there was the warmth she liked to feel in the sun on her back; the huge, deep-pink flowers on the rhododendron at the gate of the big house were open now, where they had been only in bud when she last came.

It seemed more than a fortnight ago. She had been sorry to miss last Tuesday's money, but no doubt the house would be quite tidy, if Mrs Pritchard had been away and her husband was still in Spain.

When she could not get in, she was at first irritated and then alarmed. There was post in the letter box; it was most unlike Mrs Pritchard not to have taken it in by now. Mrs Evans walked round the house, peering through windows and trying the back door. Then she went back into the lane and trudged the two hundred yards to the next house, where she got the Jacksons to ring the police.

She was pleased and secretly surprised by the speed with which they arrived. They had taken much longer to come to the burglary at her neighbour's cottage during the winter. This time, there were two constables in a patrol car there in twenty minutes, asking her questions and making her feel very important. Mrs Evans had no idea of the priority that was being given to calls like hers, as the police strove to identify a murder victim.

She met the policemen at the front door of The Beeches. She had declined the Jacksons' offer to wait for them at their house, wanting to keep all the drama of this rare moment of importance to herself. The policemen asked when she had last seen Mrs Pritchard. It was a fortnight since she had been in the house, she explained, but she had seen Mrs Pritchard in the village on the Friday of the same week, so that was ten days ago. They asked why she hadn't cleaned the house last Tuesday, and she had to explain that although she had come up here as usual, there had been a note under a stone by the front door to say that Mrs Pritchard had gone away and would not need her services until today.

She concealed the irritation she had felt at having walked up to The Beeches for nothing that day, because she felt vaguely that it would be disloyal to her employer to talk about it now. They asked if she had kept the note, and she said she thought she probably still had it somewhere at home. It gave her a little, slightly guilty thrill of excitement to tell them that. She looked up at the tall house, which seemed more silent with every passing minute of the bright morning.

She hoped that Mrs Pritchard wasn't lying dead in there. But if she was, Ivy Evans would be the only first-hand witness to tell the tale around the village. She tried not to feel too much pleasure in the anticipation; Mrs Pritchard had always been kind to her.

The policemen seemed for a moment at a loss as to what they should do. She did not expect policemen to be uncertain like this, but they did look very young. One of them had taken his hat off as the sun rose higher, and he appeared to Ivy Evans little more than a boy; she was sure also that constables had been much taller than these two when she was young.

They asked her about the Pritchards' two children, who lived away and hardly ever came here, and about Mr Pritchard. She was able to help them there, telling them of his trip to Spain with his friends from the golf club. He was away for about ten days, she thought. She wasn't sure on which day the party had gone, but it was at a weekend; a Saturday or a Sunday, she believed. They must be due back any time now.

The policeman who had kept his hat on went round to the side of the house, looking for a moment into the big greenhouse, where the plants seemed to be in dire need of water. He got out his little radio and spoke quietly into it for a few moments. The little box gave a series of harsh crackles, and then a distorted electronic voice replied to him. Mrs Evans, who would have liked to relay the conversation to her husband and her neighbours later in the day, could distinguish not a word on either side of the exchange.

The policeman came back and nodded briefly to his companion. They walked round the house, with Mrs Evans following a little way behind them. 'We shall have to get in, m' dear. You don't know where there's a spare key, do you?'

'No. I'd have got in myself, if there'd been one, wouldn't I?' She felt quite daring, ticking off policemen like that, but they were very young. He thought of telling her that the kind of people who left notes under stones on their front doorsteps to announce that the house was empty also often left keys around the place, but he didn't say anything.

She half hoped they would bring a sledgehammer and smash the lock on the big front door, as she had seen policemen do on television, but instead they broke a pane in the window of the downstairs cloakroom and reached in a hand to the catch. Then the one who had already discarded his hat took off his tunic and got in through the window. He managed to open the front door and the two policemen moved into the dark cavern of the hall.

Mrs Evans made to follow them, getting ready to act as guide to the house she knew so well, but the one who still wore his checked cap turned and stopped her. 'Best wait here for a few minutes, m' dear,' he said. 'There's no knowing what we're going to find inside, and we wouldn't want you upset. We're used to it, you see, so we're prepared for anything.'

She felt cheated for a moment. Then she consoled herself with the undeniable prospect of melodrama which his last words had carried. If her mistress—the drama had already elevated her status in the house to that of valued servant—was lying dead from a heart attack or a seizure, she would demand full details of the scene. If Mrs Pritchard had been killed by intruders, she would thrust her way past these callow young guardians to take in the full horror of the blood-soaked scene for her subsequent accounts of it.

She began to wonder if she would be featured on *Crimewatch* on the television. She would need to get her hair done.

It seemed to take the men a long time to go through the house, and the suspense built up her excitement and stretched her ever more active imagination towards new scenarios. It would have been much quicker if they had let her take them round, she thought. She did not know the cautious tread they employed and their careful, gloved handling of the doors as they moved from room to room. If there was to be a Scene of Crime team here later in the day, they did not want to blot their apprentice copybooks.

But they came out breathing more easily as they blinked at the sudden sunlight. 'No one in there, m' dear,' the one in his shirtsleeves said. She tried not to look disappointed.

He asked if she had any idea where Mrs Pritchard might be staying, and she told them sharply that if she had known that, she would have told him before he broke the window to get in. The other one went back into the house and came out with the leatherbound book the Pritchards kept beside the telephone. 'We shall need to take this with us,' he said. She didn't like it, but she supposed it was quite in order for the police to remove things from a house.

Then he asked her to help them find the children's phone numbers in the book, and she was immediately mollified. She managed to remember their first names, though she had seen the daughter only once and the son never. They managed with a little difficulty to find them in the list of numbers and addresses, their task made easier by Mrs Evans's knowledge that neither of them was local.

She rode back to the village in the police car, sitting erect and proud in the back to show any spectators that she was not under arrest. She wished it was more than quarter of a mile—she had scarcely the chance to savour the journey. They allowed her to make them a quick cup of tea, so that there was more opportunity for the village to remark the shiny white police car as it stood at her front gate.

They radioed in to tell the station that they had accompanied her home so that she could search for the note Mrs Pritchard had left for her on the previous Tuesday. For a few panic-stricken moments, whilst the policemen drank their tea and reminisced about their weekend in the kitchen at the back of the house, she thought that she had after all thrown it out with the rubbish.

Then she found it, under Mr Evans's pools coupon on the sideboard. It had her name on an envelope, like a real letter. The scrap of paper inside said only, *I'll be away this week, after all. Sorry I couldn't let you know earlier. See you next Tuesday as usual. Laura Pritchard.* It seemed strange that they should attach so much importance to a few simple words like that.

The policeman looked at it for a moment, preparing to put it carefully away inside a pocketbook in his breast pocket. He said, 'Is this Mrs Pritchard's writing? That might be quite important, you see.'

Mrs Evans understood, and felt the thrill of an awful excitement. But when she inspected the note, she had to say, 'Yes, that's her writing.' She was disappointed for the rest of the day.

## CHAPTER FOUR

Mark Warner turned the BMW out of the lane and on to the main road.

He would have driven fast on this stretch normally, pushing the needle past eighty as he reached the dual carriageway, but today he drove more soberly, easing the big car along at between fifty and sixty, where he could scarcely hear the engine note.

He had enough troubles, without being pinched again for speeding. Besides, he was in no hurry to get to this particular meeting. He drove past the freight storage depot, where he fancied he saw an air of bustling prosperity which made his own troubles seem all the more desperate. He was glad to get out on to the Bristol road, beneath a wide blue sky which made the sparse traffic seem even thinner.

He went into the works to pick up the order book. He

still kept one for his own information, though computers had long made such things obsolete. It was a small, red, linen-backed book, with handwritten entries in his flowing, confident script; the book was an exact replica of the one he had kept when they had started the business in a single Portakabin with two machines. Those had been exciting days, when new orders had come easily and the world had waited expectantly at his feet.

They had been simpler and better days too, he now decided.

The small work force tried hard to look busy when they saw that he was around, but he knew the tasks far too well to be deceived. He had worked all of the machines in the factory himself, before he afforded himself the title of managing director and left them behind. And he had been happiest when using those machines, he realized, with a shaft of the self-insight which he normally did not allow himself. In those early days, the men had been surprised to find that anyone with a university degree was so talented and well-informed about practical matters. That had made them respectful of his expertise and delighted to follow him as he developed the company.

He must not allow himself to get sentimental about the past and its successes. Something would turn up; it always had. The trouble was this damned recession, and those damned green shoots of recovery which had proved nothing more than a Chancellor's pipedream. If only bloody Laura had been prepared to help, even just a little. Just enough to reduce their borrowings, until things picked up . . . She'd have got her money back, and interest, too, if she'd wanted it.

Mothers-in-law were supposed to be obstructive though, weren't they? Well, Laura had certainly been that. And now she wasn't even there to ask. If her will left money to Joyce, that would be as good as putting it in the hands of Warner Plastics, wouldn't it? . . . Not for the first time, he thrust away that dangerously agreeable thought.

'Have Collinsons confirmed that order?' he asked Joe Brown, the senior foreman who had been glorified with the title of director. He knew the answer before he got the older man's worried negative; when there was good news, you were greeted with it at the door. He could not remember how long it had been since the last genuine good news.

He kept a bright face as he moved among the eight men who were all that remained of the twenty he had employed in the days when business burgeoned and there were nothing but compliments for the speed of his expansion and the quality of his products. It was important for morale that they should not see that the boss was worried. The quality of what they made was as good as ever, but no one could fight a demand dwindling as quickly as this.

At least he did not have to wait when he got to the bank. Cummins came out of his office immediately. He was in his late forties, with hair already silvered at the temples and a broad, rather nervous face. He held out his hand and gave Mark a broad smile. He was trying to be as pleasant as he could, but embarrassment made his bearing seem unctuous rather than friendly. Mark hoped that the half dozen people who were waiting at the counter did not notice that. The manager's 'Good to see you, Mr Warner!' seemed to him too loud and too hearty for its hollowness not to be obvious to all.

Perhaps his situation was making him over-sensitive. He sat in the armchair in front of the desk when he was invited, and tried to take the initiative. 'It's good of you to see me, George,' he said, ignoring the fact that he had been summoned here. 'Actually, I wanted a word with you about increasing our capital base.' He was a little vague about exactly what the term meant, but he had heard his accountant use it.

Perhaps he had expected in any case that he would be interrupted before he was allowed any exposition of his needs. Cummins did not look at him. He steepled his long fingers and looked at the leather-edged blotter on his desk as he said, 'There can be no question of that at present, I'm afraid, Mr Warner. Unless, of course, you are able to report a sudden upturn in business?' His grey eyebrows arched hopefully upwards.

Mark was not a fool. He knew that the manager's refusal to respond to his attempt to use Christian names was even more sinister than this question to which the man already knew the answer. He said, 'Not just yet, I'm afraid.'

Cummins gave a slight, sudden shake of his grey head, which was almost a nervous tic; it reminded Mark Warner of the way his cat refused food it did not fancy. 'That's what I feared. In fact, I asked you to see me today because it looks as though we are going to have to do something about the situation at Warner Plastics.' He always used the full name of the company. It made it less of a personal attack.

'We'd like to do something ourselves. We can't go and drag customers in by the scruff of their necks.'

'No.' Cummins had stopped smiling, and he did not begin again even in response to the nervous grin with which Warner accompanied this thought. 'It's because of that that the bank has now to give attention to your accumulating debt, Mr Warner.'

Mark swallowed hard and kept smiling. Don't let him get away with that—take the fight to him. But keep it light, he told himself. It was an impossible brief, but he tried. 'You were happy enough to advance us the money for the new factory, George. I came and took your advice, and you positively encouraged us to expand our production and move on from our old premises.'

Cummins smiled. It was an undertaker's professional smile. 'It looked the right advice at the time. On the figures you provided. The ultimate decision to expand was yours, of course. All the bank did was to offer the facilities for you to do so.'

'Facilities which apparently you are now trying to remove.'

Cummins said, 'You took a commercial decision, Mr Warner. You can't blame the bank because it now turns out to have been ill-advised.' He did not pause to consider that the advice had been his.

He had been conducting interviews like this for weeks now. He knew the tactics: always use 'we' and not 'I'; keep using the bank as big brother behind you, as though it wasn't you personally who had offered the loans, and it wasn't you personally who was now calling them in. He held all the cards; the succession of small businessmen he had been seeing were ultimately dependent on his decision, and they knew it as well as he did.

He was sorry for Warner, and others like him, who had been encouraged to expand at the wrong time and then forced to pay rates of interest they had never anticipated just as their profits slumped. But it was not his fault; not even the bank's fault. Everyone knew that the Treasury and the government were responsible, but they were the people who never picked up the tab.

And his own job was on the line now. Those borrowers who could pay were scrambling to get rid of their debts; those who could not were becoming the focus of bankers' apprehension. The message was coming down from above: foreclose on the dodgy borrowers, while they still have some assets left. Or watch out for your own job when your assessment came up.

He opened the folder in front of him and took out the sheet of paper his secretary had brought to him on the previous afternoon. 'Your debt has been accumulating. It is now approaching two hundred thousand.'

'You have increased interest rates three times since we agreed the overdraft facility. Without those rises, the overdraft would have remained static, or even gone down a little.'

Cummins waved his hands a little, palm upwards and one on each side of his body; it was a gesture he had practised thoroughly over the last month. Pilate, he thought, might have made a good banker. 'That may be true. But the rises were outside our control, Mr Warner.'

'Our turnover was still well over a million in the last financial year, despite the recession, and—'

'And what will your profits be this year, Mr Warner? We must look forwards, not backwards.'

Cummins had spoken sharply, more sharply than was intended or needed. The fact that he didn't like what he was doing, that even the good banker who still lurked within him did not approve it, made him only the more harsh. He wanted to get this over as quickly as possible.

Mark Warner knew now what was coming. He saw that his arguments were useless, and felt the net being drawn in around him. His palms and his forehead felt damp, yet his spine felt a sudden cold that made him want to shiver. He could not remember feeling thus since he was a schoolboy hauled into the headmaster's office. He felt now as he had felt then, like a fish that had been netted. Only the last, ritual thrashings were left to him as the meshes tightened.

'We've got a sound business. You said so yourself, when you advanced us the loan. It's only a matter of time before things pick up.' Warner's bright blue eyes challenged the man opposite him to deny it.

Cummins had heard those arguments too often in this room. Yet this time he was pierced by a shaft of sympathy he could not afford to show. Warner was right: his plastics business was a good one, soundly managed and with products which would be much in demand once other businesses around him picked up. Before the latest guidance came through from head office, with its scarcely veiled threats to his own position, he would never have even considered conducting this interview. Now he looked only for the weaknesses in the position of the client who had become an opponent. He said, 'Would it be correct to assume that Warner Plastics will show a loss rather than a profit in the current year?'

Warner drew both hands involuntarily through his fair

hair. It was a gesture which surprised him, because he thought he had eliminated it; he could not remember making it since he was a nervous adolescent. His fellow students had mocked it in a university sketch, and he had taken pains to get rid of it when he went into the more dangerous world outside. He said, 'Probably there will be a small loss, yes. It depends on outstanding payments due to us. But surely—'

'And what is the state of your order book?' Cummins knew that if it was healthy, that would have been displayed to him long before now.

Mark prevented himself just in time from producing the little red book. It wouldn't do to bring out such a document in this panelled shrine to commercial efficiency. Besides, the contents were not impressive. This bastard wasn't going to back off, but he must go through the motions: he might yet mitigate the severity of the sentence. 'Our order book is as healthy as anyone could expect in the present climate. Our regular customers are still with us, but of course, they're running down stocks before they re-order. We're at the stage where they're going to have to place new orders very soon now. New customers aren't easy to come by, but given a little time—'

He was aware that his words were coming ever more quickly, as he pressed on, fearful of interruption. Now he had produced the word which allowed Cummins to break in. 'Time, yes. That is a factor which is not elastic, Mr Warner. I have encouraged head office to be patient, but they point out that we must also be discreet. Once lent, twice shy, they say.' He could see that Warner did not understand that latest bit of banking jargon—indeed, he was not sure that he comprehended it fully himself. 'We managers are being forced to take a hard look at any debts which are likely to become bad ones. I'm afraid yours has been put in that category.'

'You mean *you've* put it in that category.'

'If you like, yes. But you must understand that we have been given certain guidelines, and—'

'Then let me talk to the people who gave you the guidelines. I'll show them that my business must be supported, within any reasonable "guidelines" they like to apply.'

'I'm afraid that isn't possible.' Cummins's anxious, lined face shut as suddenly as a book behind the phrase. 'And it wouldn't in any case be productive.' He knew he was right there: his superiors would support him, even if they thought he was wrong, in the present climate. What was one more small business going to the wall, among so many? More to the point, who was going to stick his neck out for someone like Warner, when so many loans were becoming bad ones?

He clasped his hands on the desk in front of him and said with an attempt at conciliation, 'I'm not saying we're trying to close you down. We want to encourage enterprise, not stifle it.' That rang hollow, even to him. He thought how much easier his job had been a few years ago, when his superiors had been encouraging him to thrust loans at anyone who wanted them. Including Warner: he remembered with a pang of remorse how anxious he had been to offer Warner finance, how worried lest this man might borrow not from him but from some other source.

Mark thought again about that order he was hoping to get from Collinsons. Maybe he should have rung them again before he came here. But he had not known then how vital it would be. He said dully, 'Exactly what are you saying then, George?'

Cummins took a deep breath, looking down again at the sheet he had taken from the folder, to give himself a little time. 'We're looking to you to make a substantial reduction in your overdraft. If you can show us that there is no need for the bank to worry about the debt in the medium term, we'll be able to discuss—'

'How quickly?'

It was nearly over now. Cummins, studying the open, defeated face on the other side of his desk, knew that the man had accepted it. 'We need to see the debt halved within three months. Cut down below a hundred thousand.'

'That isn't possible. You know it isn't possible. Not in a recession like this one.'

Cummins did his little palm-upwards gesture with his hands again, indicating how helpless he was against his draconian masters. 'I'm sorry. It has to be possible. Perhaps you can make some more economies—'

'That's impossible!' For a moment, the full torrent of Warner's frustration and resentment seemed about to burst out; like many men with fierce tempers, he had no range between apparent calmness and the full fury of rage. Then he controlled himself and spoke coldly and evenly. 'We're down to a skeleton staff of specialists already. We've cut every corner we can in production without sacrificing the quality of the product. Our margins are far too small, but if we try to increase them we shall lose what business we have.'

It was catch twenty-two, and Cummins went for it. 'I accept all of that. But it just shows why we're having to take the action I've announced to you. If you can't make ends meet even with the economies you've already made and you can't increase margins, then the bank must safeguard its investment and prevent you from getting further into debt. If you can show us your capacity to reduce your debt, then in due course—'

'And what if we can't?'

This time Cummins allowed himself a little shrug of the shoulders beneath the cloth of his lightweight suit. 'Then we should have to foreclose, I'm afraid, and safeguard our loan by the sale of your assets.' He stood up and moved round the desk; now that his message was complete, the sooner the interview was terminated, the better. 'But I hope it will not come to that, Mark. I'm sure you'll come up with something. In the meantime, I shall assure head office that you are making every effort . . .'

The emollient, meaningless phrases poured out for a few more seconds. It was only when Mark Warner was standing dazed on the pavement outside the bank that he realized that Cummins had finally addressed him by his first name.

Mark did not go back to the Warner Plastics factory immediately. He could not face the anxious dependent faces there until he had composed himself. He bought himself a pint of bitter in the old pub on the high street; the rejection of the gin and tonic which was now more normal for him was a harking back to those happier days when he had worked so hard and so successfully to build up the business.

It was a good business, with an excellent reputation. Could it really now be in such danger? Gradually, as he sipped his beer and munched his way savagely through the crisps he had allowed himself, a measure of his natural optimism returned. Something would turn up. He had always been able to make things happen, and he would do that now. He still had a few irons in the fire.

But he could think of only one source from which this sort of money might come.

He drove slowly back to the works. At least Cummins had not suggested he sell the BMW, he thought bitterly. He would have had to reveal that it was only on lease. He went quickly through his own office after parking underneath the bold 'Warner Plastics' sign, taking care not to catch the eye of any of his employees.

There was a note on his desk from his secretary, telling him that his wife had phoned. Normally she would have told him as he came through her office, or buzzed him with the news on the intercom. Today she obviously preferred the less personal contact: he wondered just how much his workers knew about the firm's situation. Probably quite a lot: they were not stupid, the people he employed, he thought, with a fierce and pointless pride. One of his projects would bear fruit. There must be a way out of this, for their sake as well as for his.

He took a deep breath before he rang his wife, bracing himself to meet her concern. He would prefer to tell her about the bank interview at home, tonight, but if she asked him he would not be able to hold back the news.

There was no need for him to have worried about that. He said, 'Joyce, it's me,' as soon as she picked up the phone, and knew even from her breathing that something was wrong.

'Mark, the police are here. It isn't the children.' He hadn't thought it would be, but her mother's heart had presumed that his thoughts, like hers, would fly to them. 'It's—it's my mother. They've found her. At least, they think it's her.'

A voice at the other end of the line said 'Mrs Warner,' and then there were exchanges too muffled for him to hear. He heard a door close and a hand pick up the receiver; he could picture the policeman at the phone in the hall, checking carefully that the door of the lounge was closed and that his wife could no longer hear the conversation.

'Mr Warner? I'm afraid we have what may be bad news for you, as you've probably gathered from your wife. We have no certainty yet about the identity, but a body has been discovered which may well be that of your mother-in-law.'

He felt his heart thumping so loudly that he switched the phone foolishly to his other hand, lest it pick up the note from his chest. 'Where was this? At home?' His voice was unsteady, he knew, but that would surely be expected by the policeman.

He was glad this news was coming to him over the phone. That should make it easier to conceal the wild mixture of hope, excitement and guilt which pounded in his head.

The calm, concerned, voice said, 'No. I'm afraid the body was found in the Severn, sir. It had been there for some time.'

'Mrs Pritchard had drowned?' He was forcing himself to say the right things, to suppress the wild optimism which was pouring now through his veins. He wondered if he was conveying the right degree of concern, but he was far too excited to estimate how he sounded.

The voice in his ear said, 'I couldn't be sure about the cause of death. The point is, sir, that we need an identification of the body, as soon as possible. I wonder if you could—'

Some impulse, part guilt, part fear, made him say, 'But doesn't the next of kin usually do that? I'm sure my wife—'

'Yes, sir. It is usually the next of kin we prefer to do the identification, for obvious reasons.' The voice was calm, practised, concerned. Then it was suddenly lowered, and Mark could imagine the man looking round again to check on the door of the lounge. 'Unfortunately, the body has been in the water for some days, as I said, sir. It is a little—er—disfigured, and we thought in the circumstances that it might be better to shield Mrs Warner from ... She's already quite upset, as you can imagine.'

'Of course. I'll do it. As soon as you like.' He hoped that he did not sound too eager.

But all the policeman said was, 'That's very good of you, sir. I think it would be best. Of course, it may not be your mother-in-law at all.'

But as Mark put down the phone and tried to breathe evenly, he knew it was. He felt now that he had been waiting for a week for just this moment: for the body of Laura Pritchard to be discovered.

Something had turned up, as he had known it would.

## CHAPTER FIVE

Sergeant Bert Hook moved around The Beeches like a burglar rather than a policeman.

Although he had been in the force for over twenty years, and in the CID for thirteen of them, he had never got rid of the feeling that exploring other people's houses without their permission was an intrusion. Even when their absence had been confirmed as permanent, as Mrs Laura Pritchard's seemed to have been by the initial comparisons of her dental records with Cyril Burgess's autopsy findings.

Hook moved his heavy frame silently about the place, treading carefully upon his large feet, as if he were in a chapel of rest rather than an empty house. The afternoon sun streamed in through the windows of the big drawing-room, and Lambert had opened a window to let in some air, but Bert still entered each room like an intruder. Perhaps it was a hangover from his days in the Barnardo's home where he had grown up: the middle classes still disturbed him a little, particularly worthy middle-class ladies like the ones who had interviewed him as an adolescent.

And this residence was eminently a middle-class one. From the thick fitted carpets of the downstairs rooms to the heavy brass light fittings of the bedrooms into which Bert reluctantly followed his chief, the big detached house spoke of comfort, even opulence. Money had not been spared here; that was especially apparent to a policeman who had married late and was finding out how expensive two young boys could be, as they went through shoes as though waging a personal war upon them.

'I still can't help feeling we should have someone's permission to be here,' Bert said to his superintendent, as he watched him picking up family photographs and opening drawers.

Lambert looked at him with a mixture of amusement and irritation, like a bold schoolboy rejecting the views of a priggish companion. 'The daughter knows we're here, Bert. The husband isn't here to ask, more's the pity. Tomorrow, the Coroner's Court will confirm the cause of death as "Murder by person or persons unknown". It behoves us to get on with it.'

He would have been sharper with a younger officer. But he had worked with Hook for ten years now, and he knew the talents beneath that rubicund, village-bobby exterior. It was worth being patient with the odd quirk of temperament to have those talents beside him. Hook's strength was with people, not things, though he could be painstaking enough with searches when it was necessary.

As if determined to thrust aside his reservations, Hook now said, 'There's no sign of a break-in, or of violence. It doesn't look as if she was killed here.'

'Maybe not. But from what we know of this death, it doesn't seem that there was a lot of blood involved. And it may be that if the killer was alone in the house with her, he had ample time to clear up at his leisure, knowing that he would not be disturbed.'

'Or that she would not be.' Hook entered the detective's automatic caveat against unwarranted assumptions.

'Exactly. No great physical strength is needed with a throat ligature. Especially if the victim is taken unawares.'

The bedrooms were as tidy as if Mrs Evans had cleaned them that day, instead of having been prevented from entering the house by the two young policemen. Too tidy, perhaps, for a woman who had been surprised and killed in the house. Perhaps she had left it neat when she left to go off somewhere. Perhaps the murderer had coolly tidied up whilst the corpse awaited removal downstairs. Lambert shook his head; speculation was useless until they knew a lot more about the woman who had been Laura Pritchard.

The sooner they could gather information from her family and friends, the sooner they would begin to get a clear picture about the character and habits of the victim. She had been dead now, it seemed, for over a week. The trail was already colder than any detectives would have liked it. And here was Bert Hook pussyfooting about intruding on people's privacy.

Lambert went back downstairs and into the lounge. He picked up the biggest photograph of the three on the sideboard. It showed a man of about fifty with a woman who looked a little younger. These were presumably Laura

Pritchard and her husband. The couple were formally dressed, he in a dark suit with a rose on his lapel and she in a two-piece with a straight skirt. There was a church in the background and they were holding themselves stiffly, their smiles a touch embarrassed, as people were when they were made to wait for a photograph with others around them.

He realized that what he had supposed from a distance to be an informal picture was almost certainly a photograph taken at a wedding. But whose? Was it Laura Pritchard who was being married? If so, it was almost certainly a second wedding for her; they already knew of the existence of a daughter and a son. Statistically, this picture was most likely to have been taken at the wedding of one of these children. But if so, the man with his arm round the dead woman might be a brother or a brother-in-law as easily as a husband.

He looked hard at the face of the woman. She had carefully waved light brown hair framing her face, but for this formal occasion the arrangement spoke more of her coiffeur's skills than of her own taste. The photographer had made her wait a little too long for his shutter, so that her smile had a glassy concentration. But she looked happy enough. Her round face was almost unlined, and the eyes were creased in what looked like genuine amusement and pleasure. Her nose was a touch small; it was a pretty rather than a classically beautiful face. The straight lines of her suit emphasized rather than disguised a good figure.

She stood erect, a little over average height; her high heels brought the top of her elegantly arranged hair almost level with that of the man next to her. She had her right arm beneath his, and her left one rather stiffly at her side, as if the photographer had told her to put it there and made her a little self-conscious. Studying the picture, Lambert was suddenly sure that she had had both hands clasped together around the man's elbow a moment earlier, but had felt or been told that the gesture was a little too proprietorial.

He looked for a moment at her feet, small and elegant beneath calves and ankles which were improved by the high heels, and tried not to think about the image his brain retained from the post-mortem table a couple of hours earlier, when those ankles were blackened by the bruising of the ropes and the feet half removed by the attentions of the creatures of the Severn.

The man in the picture was a possible murderer, as was anyone who had been in contact with the dead woman, until they could prove otherwise. His dark hair was turning grey, and receding into a baldness that was not unbecoming, adding as it did to his air of distinction. He held himself erect; he was probably about five feet ten or eleven, and quite heavily built—there was plenty of white-shirted chest visible between the lapels of his dark blue jacket. But the formality of both his dress and his pose concealed more than it revealed. It was not as though he had chosen to stand like that, Lambert realized glumly. His smile was a commanded smile, and he had the air of a man suffering a picture he knew must be taken rather than a volunteer for the album.

He did not even look at the woman next to him, but stood almost to attention with his hands straight at his sides, as if the woman who had her hand lightly beneath his elbow was no more than an appendage to a picture of him. But nothing of arrogance or indifference could be deduced from that. Many men were awkward with the formal photographs at weddings, especially if they had to hold a smile amid the raillery of their fellows. This man might have turned laughing to his partner as soon as the photographer had signified that he was released from duty. Fashions in wedding apparel change but slowly and there was no indication of how long it was since this picture had been taken.

The other photographs in the room were just as conventional. There was one of a serious-looking young man against the background of an old building; it looked as if it had been taken in a college, but there were no degree robes to indicate final examinations. Beside it was a picture of a young woman holding a shawled baby in her arms at what was probably a christening ceremony—there was another, more modern church in the background of this picture.

Hook appeared at the door of the French window; he had been looking around the immaculate gardens. 'The lawns have been cut in the last forty-eight hours,' he said. 'If the gardener comes two or three times a week, he might be able to tell us how long the place has been empty. There's no sign of any struggle in the garden.'

There were two cars in the big brick double garage, a blue Jaguar and a Vauxhall Astra. There was a bill for a full service lying face upwards on the front passenger seat of the Jaguar. Lambert glanced at the mileage recorded for the time of the service, then at the mileage at the bottom of the speedometer. They were within six miles of each other: presumably the distance between the garage and this house. He said to Hook, 'How far from here to the nearest point on the river?'

'I'd have to look at the Ordnance Survey to be sure. Not less than seven or eight miles I'd say, even by the shortest route.' So Laura Pritchard's body had not taken its last journey in this Jaguar. It was beginning to look as if she had not been murdered here. But they must be sure. And in any case, they would have to start the investigation from here.

Lambert said, 'Better tell Rushton to get the Scene of Crime boys to go over the house. We might at least learn something more about the victim and the people she knew.'

While Hook went to the other side of the house and used his radio, he looked dutifully round the garage. There was a work-bench at the far end, and the wall was covered with tools and materials on shelves and hooks. Among them were several coils of rope and thick wire.

But there would be similar things in several hundred garages within twenty miles of The Beeches.

The mortal remains of Laura Pritchard had been tidied up by the time Mark Warner arrived to inspect them.

That was the mortician's euphemism for depositing the organs which had been investigated back within the shell of the trunk and sewing that casing hastily together. It was always a little easier to reassemble the head of a woman, for the hair enabled the repairer to disguise the line where the top of the skull had been removed to examine the brain.

The work had been assigned to Binns, Cyril Burgess's young and lugubrious laboratory assistant. He surveyed his efforts with some satisfaction and decided that he had done the best job that was possible with the materials assigned to him. That did not mean that what was under the sheet was in any way a pretty sight. Binns wondered what those old cheats at the funeral parlour would be able to achieve on this one, with their embalming fluid, perfumes and cosmetics. It would be interesting to see; but see he never would. People would consider that morbid.

Binns sometimes thought he never would understand human behaviour: it was probably as well that his calling ensured that he spent most of his day working with cadavers.

Mark Warner, driving into the almost empty car park of the mortuary in the late afternoon, was beset with his own problems. The chief of these was a feeling of guilt: he could not thrust down the exultation which had been rising in him throughout the journey. He had never been very close to his mother-in-law. There had been no open quarrel, but that had been because he had shied away from one.

He had always felt that she would have preferred someone better for her daughter—a professional man, perhaps. He knew that she had been dismayed when he went back to the shop floor after a university education, even though it was his own shop floor and he had been for several years very successful. She had seemed almost gratified by his recent setbacks: now she was to be the unwitting instrument in the rescue of Warner Plastics.

But he was also troubled by something more immediate and more absurd. It was none the less disturbing for being quite trivial. He had realized only in the last mile of his journey that he was coming here to identify his mother-in-law. And with that thought, every music hall cliché of the situation had crowded in upon him. He was a man who in normal circumstances could never remember jokes. Now it seemed that every comedian's sally he had ever heard on the subject of mothers-in-law came vividly back to him. He ended up giggling nervously as he parked the big BMW, not from amusement at the jokes but at the black humour of his own situation.

Mark did not understand very much about shock.

He introduced himself to Binns, who seemed to be the only man still in the building, without really looking at him. That was just as well, for in his present state of emotion, there would have been a danger of him laughing outright. With his long, pale, melancholy face, his gaunt wrists that poked out from the too-short sleeves of his green overalls, his nervous habit of delivering every sentence in a monotone, Binns was every inch the stage straight man for abattoir humour.

His sense of propriety denied him any trace of a smile, even to welcome those who had come to complete the grim task of viewing the remains of relatives. He filled in a form and said to Warner, 'You have to sign this at the bottom to confirm the identification.'

Mark leaned forward, reaching for the pen.

'Afterwards,' said Binns. He rose and led the way through a door behind his office without any further preamble.

Binns was not after all the only man on the premises. A policeman appeared silently at Warner's side, deferential and considerate. Mark was not quite sure whence he had come, nor why he was there. Then he realized that his presence must mean that the police suspected that there was foul play involved in this death. Mark thought automatically of that phrase, avoiding the more brutal word it was meant to disguise. *Murder*. He wondered how much of this they had revealed to Joyce.

It was only when Binns had unlocked the small square door and eased the body out from its steel box on silent runners that he remembered the need to warn this visitor. 'I'm—I'm afraid she isn't all she might be, sir. She'd been in the water a long time when she was found, you see, and there—there was certain damage to the remains.'

His sigh made it sound like a complaint about the mortician's lot. He stood with both hands on the cloth which covered the corpse, waiting for the signal to go ahead. Having arrived at this point, Mark suddenly wanted to delay the moment of confrontation with the features he fancied he could already see in outline beneath the sheet. Suppose that this body which they had fished out of the river was not after all Mrs Pritchard? How would he react then? If this was not the face he was expecting to see, the response expected of him would be one of relief. Yet he felt sure he would show disappointment. He would feel like a man thrown a lifeline who then finds it withdrawn before he can grasp it.

In that cold room, he was aware of his palms hot and damp again, as they had been earlier in the day in the bank manager's office. Even the policeman and this strange fellow who had brought him into the place seemed to be looking at him curiously. But surely they must see all kinds of reactions in here.

Mark said, in a curiously hoarse voice that sounded in his ears like someone else's, 'OK. I'm ready.'

He should have heeded Binns's warning. He was not prepared for the missing eye, nor for the damage done to the cheek beneath the socket by a creature he tried not to envisage at its work. Binns had done his best to conceal things with the damp hair, but he had had to drape it in opposite directions to cover the marks of the autopsy work on the skull and the earlier ravages of nature. The hair gave a curious, doll-like look to the damaged head, as though some destructive child had made a clumsy attempt to conceal her mischief from her parents.

But at least it was Laura Pritchard. There was enough of the face left for Mark Warner to be quite sure of that. He took a deep breath and said steadily, 'Yes. That is Mrs Pritchard.' Then he went back into the office and signed the form to confirm it.

Mark wondered what else he should say to show the proper degree of concern. He said a little desperately, 'She wasn't—interfered with, was she? Sexually, I mean?'

It felt awkward, but it was probably the right inquiry, for Binns seemed to be half expecting it. He said, 'I understand not, sir.'

Binns was not a man for conversational niceties, so Mark was able to get away to the car almost immediately. He sat there for a few minutes, gathering his thoughts. It was the first pause for reflection he had given himself since he had heard the news.

The police Panda car was already disappearing; it had been left discreetly on the other side of the mortuary, away from the public parking spaces. Mark watched Binns come out and drive away in his ageing Fiesta, studiously avoiding any look towards the BMW lest he embarrass a relative who might be disturbed by the experience he had undergone. It was the mortician's first concession towards diplomacy.

Mark sat undisturbed for a little while longer. In a few minutes, he must be on his own way, but there was no real urgency. Joyce would know in her heart by now that her mother was dead; there was no harm in letting the news sink in before he returned home. It was important that when he got there, he should be suitably grave and sympathetic towards her grief. As he turned the key and started the engine, he hastily put on the car radio. Any programme would suffice to drown that curious, unnerving sound, which he had thought for a moment could not be coming from him.

It was the sound of hysterical laughter.

## CHAPTER SIX

The man in the photograph with Laura Pritchard was indeed her husband.

Lambert knew that as soon as he saw the party coming from the plane. There were four of them, made into an obvious group by the golf clubs they had just collected from the carousel with the rest of their luggage. Pritchard was the dominant one, making some joke which Lambert and Hook could not hear as they waited at the barrier, turning to see the reactions of the smiling men alongside him. He had grown a two-inch wide black moustache since the photograph was taken, and his hair had receded a little further, but otherwise he was an animated version of the man frozen into self-conscious stillness by the photographer at the wedding.

'Mr James Pritchard? We're police officers, sir. We need to have a word with you.'

'What've you been up to, Jim? I told you you were being watched with that barmaid!' said one of his companions, and the others greeted the standard joke with the standard guffaws. They were self-consciously cheerful; no doubt they had made a determined attack upon the charter flight's duty-free drinks.

Lambert said, 'Would you come with us please, Mr Pritchard?' and led him away to the interview room set aside for him by the airport police. Hook walked alongside Pritchard and studied him closely as they followed Lambert, looking for any initial signs that waiting detectives were half expected by the dead woman's spouse.

Pritchard passed that preliminary examination—he seemed genuinely puzzled by their presence.

He dropped his golf clubs and his suitcase awkwardly into the limited space, then sat on one of the upright chairs which were all the room afforded in the way of seating. Lambert and Hook sat facing him, no more than five feet away. Both interviewers and their subject found themselves without the protection which a desk always seems to afford. Lambert, studiously low-key, said, 'I'm afraid we have bad news for you. It's your wife, Mr Pritchard.'

'Is she ill? Has there been some kind of accident?' They were watching him unashamedly. Ordinary people might have turned away, from embarrassment or a wish to respect the man's privacy at the moment of this announcement. But these were policemen, engaged in what they were already sure was a murder investigation, and this man might well know more than he ought to do about his wife's death.

In this small, windowless cell, he was like a specimen under a microscope, and they might never have so good an opportunity to study his behaviour under stress. His clothes carried the smoke of the aeroplane into the small room; he and his friends had been confined in the ever-shrinking section for those who indulged. But there was no sweat apparent upon him. They could smell the whisky on his breath, but there was no sign now that his senses were blunted by alcohol. Lambert said quietly, 'I'm afraid your wife is dead.'

Pritchard's dark eyes widened. The line which ran up into his forehead from the top of his nose grew deeper. He uncrossed his knees and clasped his hands upon his lap. If he had expected this news, he had prepared himself well, for he certainly appeared shocked by it. He said stupidly, 'Are you sure?' And then, realizing the banality of that question before they could answer it, 'How did it happen? Was it a road accident? She'd had her car serviced not long before I went away—'

'It wasn't a road accident, Mr Pritchard. Her body was found in the river Severn two days ago.'

'Drowned? But she never went near open water. She was quite a strong swimmer, but even when we were on holiday she would only swim in the hotel pool.'

A waitress in the airport livery came rather self-consciously into the room with a brown tray and the three cups of tea that Lambert had arranged she should bring. No one said anything until she had left; the few seconds seemed to stretch out to a much longer interval.

They watched James Pritchard balancing his saucer carefully on his knees, opening the little packet of white sugar and putting half of it carefully into the cup, for all the world as if he had just been told that his wife had a cold. His hands shook a little—Lambert realized with irritation that these reactions would fit a bereaved husband in shock as easily as a murderer who knew he was under scrutiny.

When the door had shut behind their waitress and they were alone again, he said, 'Your wife did not drown, Mr Pritchard. She was already dead when she went into the water.'

'But—look, Mr Lambert, if you're trying to say that Laura committed suicide, you're barking up the wrong tree. She's never—'

Interesting, that reaction. Most people, given the bare fact he had just released, would have jumped at foul play rather than suicide. But perhaps Laura Pritchard had contemplated suicide at some time, or even attempted it. 'We're not suggesting that, Mr Pritchard. There will be a Coroner's Inquest in the next couple of days. But I have to tell you that we are treating your wife's death as a suspicious one.'

Pritchard looked at Lambert with his mouth open, frozen for a moment in shock. His cup was not quite straight, and a tiny rivulet of tea began to dribble unremarked into the saucer. Hook leaned forward almost apologetically and straightened it; Pritchard looked down at it stupidly. He said 'Murder? But who would want to . . . ?"

That at any rate was a standard reaction. Lambert said quietly, 'At present, we've no idea. Mr Pritchard, I realize that this has come as a great shock to you, but we need your help. I'm sure that you will be as anxious as we are that the person who killed your wife is arrested as soon as possible. Do you feel up to answering a few questions?'

Pritchard looked at him dazedly for a moment, as if he still could not comprehend the news. Then he said, 'Yes. Of course I want to help.' He looked round the small, hot room in bewilderment for a moment, as if taking it in for the first time. He seemed suddenly diminished from the dominant man they had collected at the barrier; he looked now like a confused child in search of a familiar face. He said abruptly, 'Look, we're all supposed to be going home in Charlie Baker's car. We came together, you see, and parked in the long-term car park . . .'

It was not necessarily insensitivity in him. Often in shock it was the small, practical things which took over, as though the mind seized on something it could deal with in order to turn away from the unthinkable. Hook said, 'Your friends are having a cup of tea in the buffet. They'll wait for half an hour; if we're not through by then, we'll see that you get home, Mr Pritchard. Or to wherever you want to go for tonight.'

Jim Pritchard seemed puzzled at the suggestion that he might not want to go back to The Beeches. Lambert said, 'Did your wife drive you to Mr Baker's house on the morning you left for Spain?'

'No. Charlie picked us all up from home, me first and then the others. We all live within a few miles of each other.'

'Was your wife at home when you left?'

'Yes. Originally I'd planned that she'd drive us to the airport in her car, but four of us and all our gear would have been too much of a squash. Charlie has a Range Rover, you see, and we piled everything into that.'

'And that, of course, was the last time you saw your wife.'

'Yes.' For a moment he looked as if he was going to break down. The large teeth of his upper jaw pulled at his lower lip and he gripped his hands into two hard fists in his lap. Hook hastily removed the now empty cup and saucer from his knees.

Lambert said, 'This will seem a foolish question. But I want you to answer it carefully, because it's a very important one. Are you aware of anyone who might have wanted to kill your wife?'

Pritchard's broad face clouded with concentration; it was so much that of a boy dutifully observing some adult command that Lambert wondered whether there was really much thought going on behind it. 'No. Laura hadn't—' He stopped himself, and looked at them with a tight smile, as if waiting for a reaction. 'I was going to say that she hadn't an enemy in the world, but I expect everybody says that.'

'Quite a few,' said Lambert. His small, answering smile was like a bait to tempt a fish.

'Anyway, it wouldn't be true. Laura could be sharp. Not everyone liked her. But no one disliked her enough to kill her.'

'But we don't yet know whether the mind involved in this was entirely rational, you see, Mr Pritchard. Had your wife had any recent disputes or arguments that you are aware of?'

'Not serious ones. She had a few words with the chap who does our gardening, I gather. I wasn't there at the time. But I'm sure—'

'What was the cause of that?'

'Well, as I say, I wasn't present; it was when I was at work. But while he's willing enough and a good worker, he doesn't know too much about gardening, and Laura does.' He slipped into the present tense in a way that was entirely natural for a man not yet accustomed to his bereavement, and went on without apparently noticing it. If he was acting, he was doing it very well. 'I think he pulled out some things as weeds which turned out to be seedlings Laura had left deliberately. But I'm not sure, you'd need to ask him. What I am sure about is that it wasn't a killing matter—the lad didn't even lose his job.'

Lambert noted with interest that they had a young male as gardener at The Beeches. And that he had had a dispute with the deceased. 'Are you aware that your wife had any other enemies? Bear in mind that we are starting from the beginning in this, and things that seem insignificant at this stage may well turn out to be quite crucial. Were there any arguments within the family?'

Pritchard stared for a moment into space, his dark eyes seeming as though they looked well beyond the plain cream walls of the small room. 'I don't know how much you know about us yet. I've been married to Laura for almost four years. It was a second marriage for both of us. Laura was divorced, and my first wife died eight years ago.'

He paused for a long time. It was only when it was apparent that he was not going to continue that Lambert said, 'Forgive me, Mr Pritchard, but in a murder investigation we need to get as full a picture as we can as quickly as we can. Was the marriage a happy one?'

For the first time, Pritchard looked angry. His dark eyes narrowed and they heard his breath drawn in quickly through tightened lips. Then he controlled himself and spoke quietly, as if determined to keep his resentment under control. 'Yes, I think so.' He stopped again for a long moment and then said, like one determined to be honest, 'Perhaps it wasn't as passionate or as boisterous as both of us might have hoped at the outset. But it was happy enough, yes, for a contract made after the first bloom and optimism of youth had left us.'

It was a little too elaborate, a little too considered a judgement for one compelled upon him in these circumstances. Lambert wondered if he was preparing the ground for what they were bound to find out from others in the course of their questionings. Lambert said, 'Had you children from your previous marriages?'

'I have one boy in Australia. He's twenty-nine now. He came to the wedding, but we haven't seen him since. Laura had a son and a daughter. The son's in London—we hardly ever see him.'

Hook said, 'We haven't had a reply from his phone number yet.'

'No. He may have left that place.' Pritchard showed no surprise that they should have that number, though they had got it from the book in his house. 'Laura liked her daughter, but she thought she could have had a better son-in-law. She wasn't very keen on Mark Warner.'

'Any reason for that?'

He pursed his lips. 'I'm trying to be fair.' Whether to the dead woman or to her son-in-law, it wasn't clear. 'There was a clash of temperaments, I think. Mark was a bit full of his business success at the time when we married, and Laura thought him rather a brash young man for Joyce. In the last couple of years, Mark's business has got into trouble, and I think he might have asked Joyce to persuade her mother to help.'

'But you aren't sure of it?'

'No.' He looked full into Lambert's face. 'I said our marriage was successful, and I think it was. But we had our separate lives in many ways. I spend most of the day at work. Laura owns a secretarial agency in Worcester, but she's handed a lot of the day to day stuff over to a manager, so that she doesn't have to be there full time. Even our hobbies are different. Laura doesn't play golf, and I spend a lot of time at the club. She sings in the Cathedral Choir, and that takes up quite a lot of her time.' He had slipped back into the present tense, again without seeming to notice.

'Thank you. This may be painful, but it is helpful to us. Except where the killer is obvious or confesses, as in most domestic homicides, we begin by building up the fullest picture we can of the victim and her habits. How often did Mrs Pritchard attend the choir activities?'

'At least once a week. Sometimes two or three times, when they had a performance coming up. It was always pretty hectic at around this time and into the summer, as the Three Choirs Festival got closer.'

Lambert shrank from the thought of sifting through a choir to find who had known this woman closely. Why couldn't she have been in a folk trio or a string quartet? But he showed nothing in his expression—Pritchard saw only a long, concerned face beneath observant grey eyes and plentiful grizzled hair. 'You say that your son-in-law might have asked your wife for money in the last year. Perhaps through your daughter.'

'My step-daughter, yes.'

Was there a significance in the promptness of that correction? 'And was your wife sympathetic to this request?'

Pritchard shrugged his wide shoulders, which had lifted a little as he talked, as if the concentration this exchange was demanding of him was itself an aid in managing his grief. 'The short answer is that I don't know; we never even discussed it. But I can tell you exactly what her response would have been. There is no way Laura would have helped Mark Warner, even if he had made his request through her daughter.'

'What were your own relationships with your step-daughter and her husband, Mr Pritchard?'

Again he weighed the question, as if determined to be as objective as possible. 'I liked Joyce from the start. But they have their own young family and they live a good twenty miles away. And as I've indicated, Laura and I have—had—busy lives of our own. We've only been married four years; I feel I haven't got to know Joyce as well as I should have liked to.'

'And her husband?'

'I understand Mark Warner. I sympathize with him. He has a good business which is being destroyed through no fault of his own, but because he tried to expand at the beginning of this damned recession.'

It sounded like a prepared, slightly defensive statement. Perhaps he had made it before, in different circumstances. To his murdered wife, perhaps?

Lambert said, 'I understand that. But how did you feel towards Mr Warner personally?'

Pritchard looked a little puzzled. Then he said, 'I suppose I have always considered him as a businessman, because I'm one myself, though in a totally different field. He seems a pleasant young man, but I feel I hardly know him outside his working context. He appears to be a perfectly adequate husband and father. He didn't get on with Laura, as I've said, so I didn't see a great deal of him. And our leisure interests don't coincide.'

In other words, thought Bert Hook, busy with his notebook, the poor sod doesn't play golf. One up in Bert's book, that put Mark Warner. His chief's predilection for the game was one of the few things Bert did not approve about Lambert. The sergeant said, as if anxious to complete his record, 'Can you give us the address of this gardener you mentioned? The one who had had a dispute of some kind with your wife.'

'Oh, that was nothing that would lead to murder, I'm sure, Sergeant.' As if he realized that he was a little too much in control of himself for a bereaved husband, Pritchard shuddered suddenly, as a small, tearless sob shook his frame. They left him to recover without comment, and he said lamely, 'But no doubt you know your business.'

Lambert said, not unkindly, 'We have our procedures, at any rate, sir. Generally they work fairly well. Do you have your gardener's address?'

'Er, no, I can't recall it, I'm afraid.'

'Would this be his phone number?'

Pritchard looked down at the scrap of card with the number in Hook's round figures. 'Yes, I'm almost certain that's it.' Again he showed no surprise that they should have such information.

Lambert said, 'One thing we need to establish is when your wife was last seen alive. Do you know of any arrangements she had made to go away from home while you were abroad?'

Pritchard looked surprised. 'No. She was staying at The Beeches. She might have gone out somewhere for the day, but . . . Have you any reason to think she went away?'

Hook, at a nod from his superintendent, said, 'She cancelled the milk, sir. From Monday.'

Pritchard shook his head, as though trying to clear it in the interests of recall. 'That surprises me, I must admit. Perhaps she just found that she had too much over the weekend, once she was left on her own. Not that I drink much milk.' He made it sound like an illegal substance.

Hook said, 'But then you would probably put, "No milk today", rather than "No milk until further notice", wouldn't you?'

'I suppose you would, yes.'

The man was suddenly flat, almost exhausted. It was often the way emotional upset affected people. They asked a little more about the shadowy figure of the dead woman's son in London, but he could tell them very little. A dropout, he thought, though well enough educated. Laura had talked very little of him, even to her husband. The boy's name was Peter Brooke, from her previous marriage. They got the impression that he knew a little more than he was prepared to reveal at present.

Then they let him go. They watched discreetly as he joined his holiday companions in the reception lounge. The airport staff who had deposited the travellers there had not thought it their business to tell them about Laura Pritchard's death, so that it was Pritchard himself who had to tell them the reason for the delay.

Lambert and Hook could see the group clearly enough

from fifty yards away: behind the huge sheets of plain glass, the shadowless artificial light showed them as clearly as tropical fish. The three of them mimed their shock and concern at the news he brought them, then moved clumsily forward to offer consolation, hesitant like most British males at the prospect of physical contact with a man. One of them managed an ill-coordinated hug; the other two pumped Pritchard's hand in turn, their vigour showing how glad they were to discover a physical gesture within the bounds of their convention.

The only man who seemed to know how to behave without embarrassment in the situation was Jim Pritchard himself. But then he had known about this death longer than the others. Half an hour longer, at least.

## CHAPTER SEVEN

As Everton Smith moved out of the Social Security office, he felt the elation coursing through his veins.

He hated the smell of the place. It was not just the smell of crowded and dubiously washed humanity, he decided. There was also the suffocating smell of failure and fractured hopes hanging about the place; even the copious crystals of ammonia in the stark toilets could never prevail over these.

He'd had a long wait, as usual, and he'd never been any good at waiting; he hadn't the patience. And he'd got the usual stupid questions from the bored woman behind the desk. It wasn't worse for him because he was black—that pimply whitey behind him had had the same treatment. Perhaps the woman had been directed to ask the same series of questions of everyone; perhaps she had to do it to keep her own job.

And he had got his Giro in the end, as he had known he must. There was no work to be had by lads like him anywhere round here at present. Anywhere in the Midlands; anywhere in the country, from all he could tell. Not legitimate work, anyway, though there was a kind of employment for those who looked hard. The black economy, they called it. It had taken him a while to realize that the term had nothing to do with the colour of his skin. And that stupid woman with her questions hadn't even got near to it.

But now he had his Giro, and he was free of that place, with its smells and its hypocrisy, for another couple of weeks. He sniffed the city air as if it were the purest Alpine breeze. Soon he would be on his bike, master of himself and his destiny; at least for those precious minutes when it took all his concentration and marshalled all his sharp young skills.

He picked it up from the tight little cul-de-sac which ended against the high blank wall of the warehouse. No one had come back to the cars which flanked it like shabby bodyguards; he was relieved about that. They had been parked just far enough apart to leave him room to put his big machine in between them, but if one of the owners had come back and tried to move out, his precious bike could have been damaged. Tipped over off its stand, he shouldn't wonder—he glanced quickly at the ageing Datsun with its trimming of rust, which was within a foot of the gleaming white of his petrol tank. The car had a cheap child's car seat leaning rather drunkenly from the back seat—probably a woman driver, he decided. Lucky he'd got back before the silly cow bounced her old rust-bucket into his machine.

The Honda 750 African twin started first time, as always. The noise bounced off the high brick wall behind it, sounding in the confined space loud as an aeroplane engine. He twisted the throttle a few times before he let the clutch in, just to savour that smooth snarl of soaring decibels. He saw people looking at him disapprovingly from the end of the cul-de-sac, sixty yards away, before they hurried on. No older people wanted to tangle with young blacks nowadays. They left that to the gangs of young whites.

Everton let the engine idle for a moment, listening to the smooth four-stroke tick-over before his helmet shut out the note and he placed his gauntleted hands carefully, exactly, on the handlebar grips. He moved carefully to the end of the street and turned confidently into the stream of traffic. This bike deserved to be driven responsibly and well, and Everton Smith was the man to do it.

The one-way system meant he had to move in the wrong direction for a time, but he enjoyed showing his skills and road awareness in the traffic. Now that the Social Security had been outwitted again, he was a model citizen. He grinned at the surprise and pleasure on an elderly driver's face when he gave way to him at a roundabout. They were all right, the wrinklies, once you got to know them: sometimes he thought he liked them better than anyone.

He was using his courtesy to delay the moment of arrival at the dual carriageway, like a connoisseur savouring his preparations for the consumption of a fine wine. Even on the big roundabout, with the high green trunk road signs above him, he eased the Honda gently into its roadline, proud of the fact that he didn't need to use his brakes at all.

Then, at last, he opened the throttle as he moved on to the black tarmac of the fast road. The moment when the power leapt like a wild beast between his thighs was the best of all. He felt the bike move from twenty to sixty in five seconds as he twisted the grip, smoothly, without the snatching which threw kids into skids. Then he was into top gear, the change as soft and soundless as a mother stroking her baby's hair. Flat against the tank now, man and machine as one, his brain relaying its instructions directly to the magnificent machine it controlled.

The rear bumpers of the cars he overtook came at him quickly, almost as quickly as the backs of the cars in those videos on television, where they put a camera on a Formula

One car. He liked that comparison. There was not much traffic in the mid-afternoon. He did not stay in the outside lane, but weaved in and out as he overtook, enjoying leaning low and feeling his mastery of the great machine. He felt like a vast swallow, swooping exactly to the spots he had chosen, master of the element in which he moved.

He glanced regularly at his mirror—the good rider always knew what was behind him as well as what was ahead. You needed to watch for the pigs when you upped your speed like this, though he was confident he had not passed any of them. All he saw were the rapidly receding bonnets of the cars he had overtaken.

He eased the bike up to the ton: he always liked to touch that alluring figure when the conditions were right. The needle crept smoothly to the magic hundred, then stayed there, with the rider perfectly in control of himself and his machine. Even at this speed, he could observe the rev counter and the temperature gauge, registering exactly what they should on each side of the speedo. He enjoyed the frightened surprise which appeared briefly beside him on the face of the woman driving a new red Fiesta. For a moment he sat almost upright to smile at her from within his helmet on the unusually tall bike. Then she was gone, a receding image in his mirror, diminishing to no more than a dot before he swung into a long bend and lost her for ever.

He always enjoyed that bend. It was beautifully cambered for high speed, enabling him to lean gently with it, placing the big Honda on exactly the line he chose and holding it as the road straightened into the long bridge over the river.

He would have liked to go further, to give the smooth-running beast a real run before bedding it down for the night. He liked to think of it like that—it gave him a closer, more personal relationship with the thing he loved. But he knew he must get back to the house. He would have a couple of hours, probably, before the others came. Everton liked having time to himself; time when he could think, and make his own plans.

Once he had left the dual carriageway, he reverted to his cautious mode of riding. It was best to anticipate that there were idiots around every corner. He was not stupid enough to ignore the fact that you were vulnerable on a bike; anyway, the Honda was too precious for him to risk getting it damaged. He had worked hard to get it; and taken certain risks.

He saw the big old Vauxhall as he turned into Jackson Terrace. There were two men in it, but he didn't look at them as he went past; young black men were safer not showing too much curiosity in these streets. He eased the big machine round the back of the mean houses, moving it over the uneven cobbles of the narrow back entry at not much more than walking pace. He had to get off to open the battered, almost paintless rear door, then mount the machine again to get it into the yard—it was too heavy for him merely to push it through the three-foot gap.

But the trouble was worthwhile—once the machine was in this narrow little flagged enclosure, he felt it was reasonably safe. Left in front of the house, it would have been stolen or vandalized within hours. There wasn't another bike like it around. Its rider set it carefully on its stand, three inches from the wall as always, where he would be able to check on it through the narrow window of the room upstairs.

He was taking off his helmet when the men arrived, just as he turned to shut the shabby green door of the yard upon the world beyond it. They were dressed in suits: he did not see many people here who dressed like that. If they were villains, they could be big trouble. He moved his helmet to his left hand, but did not begin to remove his leathers; they would provide some sort of protection, if there was going to be violence.

The taller one watched him; the burly one walked over to inspect the bike, running a finger appreciatively over its distinctive twin headlamps. He said, 'They get better every year, don't they? Electric starting, a row of instruments like a car. Not like when I used to ride a Royal Enfield: that was a real bugger to start on a cold morning.'

Smith recognized that this was only the prologue; the tone was pleasant, but at any moment this talk could turn into a taunt. He said, 'Who are you?' and was surprised how thin and cracked his voice sounded on the words.

The man turned from the bike to look at him, feeling inside the pocket of his jacket. He produced not a weapon but a police warrant card, with a fading picture of himself. 'We're police officers. I'm Detective Sergeant Hook; this is Superintendent Lambert.' The taller man gave Smith a small, confirmatory smile as he turned; his eyes had not left his since they arrived.

Smith felt relief rising within him; at least he was not going to be beaten up in this quiet yard; at least his bike would be safe. He was enough a product of his environment to say disgustedly, 'Bloody pigs! I knew you were, as soon as I saw you.' It was not true; his brushes had always been with the uniformed branch, and he had never even thought that these men might be CID. But his aggression was a conditioned reaction, and one they registered as such without feeling much rancour.

Hook merely said, 'You *are* Everton Smith, of this address?'

'Yes. How'd you know that?'

Hook grinned tolerantly at his naïvety. 'We knew about the bike. Makes it easy to identify a man, a nice bike like this.' He didn't mention that they had known also about the colour of his skin, judging correctly that Smith would be a little flattered by the mention of his bike as a mark of distinction.

Smith said, 'My tax is all paid up. I've got my insurance and my licence inside, if you want to see them.' But his mind was already telling him that plain-clothes pigs didn't visit about things like that. It was Lambert—standing behind him—who said, 'We're investigating a suspicious death. We need to ask you some questions. It would be better if we went inside.'

They sat on wooden chairs and looked round the room where he led them. In the heyday of the house sixty years ago, this had probably been called a breakfast-room; there was no division between this space and the tiny kitchen with its square, cracked window overlooking the yard. The wallpaper, what there was of it, had probably been there for most of those sixty years. In the high parts of the room grimy roses stretched towards an incomplete picture rail. Above the battered skirting board, the paper had disappeared altogether, detached in strips by damp and a hundred departed hands. A single unshaded light bulb hung at an angle from its faded purple flex.

There was an ancient and greasy electric stove in the kitchen, and a sink where even the cleaning utensils looked in need of a thorough cleansing. The dish-mop which had once been white was a dark grey; the pan-scrub looked as if it would add more grease than it removed; long streaks of spilled green streaked the sides of the plastic cylinder of supermarket washing-up liquid. There were chipped mugs in a basin of cold water; grease had congealed upon its surface.

Policemen take in the detail of rooms automatically, even when they have other things on their minds. They had ample time to look at this one, for it takes a man quite a time to divest himself of good motorcycle gear. When Smith had sloughed off the black leather which covered his torso, he sat in a chair to peel off the leggings. Bert Hook said, 'Unusual name, Everton. Support them, do you?'

'No. My Dad chose the name. After the cricketer. I think *he* was named after the football team.'

Hook nodded. 'He was. I played against him once. Only in a charity match: I was never in his class.'

The boy was interested in spite of himself. 'Get him out, did you?'

Bert Hook smiled. 'No. He hit me for three sixes in one over. And not many did that, in those days.' For a moment he was back a quarter of a century, a young fast bowler in the prime of life, being put to the sword by a cricketing prince who had officially retired.

'He was good, wasn't he?' There was a shy, wondering pride in Everton that his namesake should have done such things.

'He was the best there was. Until Sobers came along, anyway. I bounced him after the first six, and he hooked me out of the ground. On to it like a black panther he was!' He could see that lightning movement now, the bat whirling so fast it became a blur, the wide white grin in the ebony face afterwards like that of a delighted small boy.

Smith was out of his leathers at last. He looked suddenly smaller, his small bones almost fragile in the cheap jeans and shirt. Obviously, he reserved his extravagance for the bike and its trappings. Hook said to him, 'Have you come from work? You're home early.'

Smith smiled wryly at the thought. 'I haven't worked for—for a while now. I've been to sign on.'

Hook looked at the narrow staircase which ran up from the shadowy hall beyond the open door. 'Do you have a room here?'

'Yeah. A small one. You can see it, if you like.' He knew now why they were here, but perhaps there was no need to worry about it. He led them up to the room; the boards creaked beneath the big men behind him, though they trod more softly than he.

It was what they would have expected. It had a narrow bed, which they noticed he had made, and a battered, drunken wardrobe. There were no drawers, and no chair; there was scarcely room for them in this tiny cell. But they recorded one important fact—he had the room to himself. Privacy, even of this limited kind, did not come cheap in the world in which Everton moved. This mean house was no squat, as at least two of the others were in this squalid street. Smith had used a key to get in, and even the downstairs bay window was not boarded up.

There was a new little pine shelf near the foot of the narrow bed. There were two photographs here; one was of a young Everton with his first bike, an old Suzuki ER 50 trail bike with patchy red paintwork. The other was of a broad-shouldered black man with his hair greying at the temples, brandishing a beer can at the camera in a cheerful toast. Lambert picked it up and looked his question.

'It's my Dad.'

'Back in Jamaica?'

Everton smiled his contempt. He was happy at the suggestion; he enjoyed the novelty of patronizing senior pigs. 'In Smethwick. He'd already been there ten years when I was born. Actually, I took that at Edgbaston. When Viv Richards was knocking England around.'

They turned to go back downstairs. Hook said, 'No mother, then, Everton?' He knew there would have been a picture on that shelf, if there was.

'No. She left when I was six.' He was ahead of them on the stairs. They could not see his face, but his voice was calm.

'How long since you lived at home, Everton?'

They were back in the bigger room at the back of the house now so that this time they saw the pain on his face. 'My Dad died last year. He—he got cancer.' His small, neat features set hard. He would not tell them about the smoking, about how he had pleaded with him to stop. That would be a kind of disloyalty. 'He was only fifty.'

He sat down abruptly at the scratched table, staring hard at its surface, as if it might reveal to him some of the mysteries of life. The two big men sat carefully opposite him, fearing that the rickety chairs might collapse beneath them. Hook said, 'How long since you worked, Everton?'

He looked up then, a little spark of fear in his dark brown eyes. 'A year. Perhaps a bit more.' The wide vowels of the West Indian speech he had inherited from his father were overlaid with the flat tones of Birmingham; it was a curious combination.

'How much do you pay for a room here?'

He knew where this was going now; he considered a lie, then rejected it. 'Thirty quid a week.' He stared sullenly at the table for a moment, then allowed his resentment to get the better of him. 'It's going up to thirty-five next week. Bloody robbery, for what we get!'

'Will you be able to pay it?'

'I'll find it. Have to. Ain't goin' back to the squat.'

'And then there's your food to pay for.' Hook glanced across to the unsavoury kitchen, where the tap dripped loud, pacing their conversation like a metronome. 'Your bike's all in order, as you said. Taxed and insured. Insurance can't come cheap on a 750, not for a lad under twenty-five. How old are you by the way, Everton?'

'Twenty-two.'

'Is the bike paid for?'

'Yes. Well, almost. I'm up to date on the payments. Ahead, in fact.' His pride in that made him reveal it, even though he knew it was leading him into deeper water.

Hook put in the knife quietly. 'Lot to support on a Giro, isn't it, Everton?'

Everton Smith sighed hopelessly. The pigs were always after you, even when they talked about bikes and cricket. How did they expect you to survive, when you were black and without proper qualifications? 'All right. I do bits of work. Ain't no thief, though.'

'I'm glad to hear it. What kind of work?'

The thin, handsome face was perplexed, not able to assess from the sergeant's impassive face just how deep was the trouble he had waded into. He looked from Hook to the long, attentive face of the man beside him, who had hardly spoken. Without their uniforms, he was not even sure which of these was the senior rank. 'I do anything that's offered. Bits of gardening. House removals, when they need an extra man. Work on cars, when I can get it.

Decorating—but they don't think us black bastards have any idea about things like that. We live in tin shacks and play the bongos.'

There was no real bitterness in his words. Whatever prejudice he had come up against, he had long ago accepted it as a fact of life. Like unemployment. Hook said, 'We know about some of your work, Everton. At Mr Pritchard's.'

He said sullenly, 'You gonna book me?'

Lambert said, 'I shouldn't think so, Everton. You cooperate with us, which won't be difficult, and we'll forget all about the bits of work. We aren't interested in what you say to the Social Security people; we're pursuing a murder inquiry. Into the death in suspicious circumstances of Mrs Laura Pritchard.'

Smith looked again from one to the other, wondering what to make of an approach he had never met before. The truth was that he had been softened up. Although he did not realize it, he was not likely to hold back anything now. There was a catch in his throat when he spoke, so that he had to begin again. 'All—all right. What do you want to know?'

He must have read about the death for he expressed no surprise. He might, of course, have been involved in it. Hook produced a notebook and said, 'How long have you been working at The Beeches?'

The young man's forehead creased into a frown. Many suspects adopted the tactic of affecting to give serious consideration to the most innocent of questions, in the hope that their prepared answers for the more important ones would be accepted at face value. But Everton Smith was not yet a serious suspect. 'It must be about nine months now. I started at the end of last summer, and they kept me on through the winter.'

'And who offered you that work?'

'Mr Pritchard. I worked for a few weeks at his golf club in August and September, filling in for the lads whilst they had their holidays. I hoped something more permanent might come of it, but . . .' His shrug encompassed the hopelessness of both that idea and life in general.

'And have the Pritchards been good employers?'

'Yes. They kept me on all through the winter. Only once a week, but I was glad of that. And now I'm back on twice a week.' Suddenly, his too-revealing face clouded with anxiety. 'Will they—will Mr Pritchard—still want me after this?'

'I'm afraid that will be up to Mr Pritchard, Everton.' He noticed how the face lightened at that thought. 'Get on well with him, do you?'

'Quite well. I hardly see him, though. Mrs Pritchard was nearly always there. She used to work with me in the garden a lot of the time. And she always paid me before I came away.'

'What days were you there?'

'Usually Monday and Friday. But she didn't mind if I varied it when I got other work, so long as I let her know.'

'How did you get on with Mrs Pritchard?'

'Well enough. She made me coffee, usually.'

They gave him the chance to enlarge on this, but he did not. It was Lambert who said quietly to him, 'We heard you had a bit of a row with her, Everton.'

He looked a little frightened now. Perhaps he had not expected them to know this. 'It wasn't anything much. I pulled out some plants I should have left, that's all. I thought they were weeds, but they were seedlings, waiting to be planted out. Sweet Williams, I think she said. We rescued most of them. They're flowering now, in the bed where I planted them.' There was a little flash of pride in his newly discovered horticultural skills.

Suddenly, there was a sound as of a parrot being strangled, and all three men jumped. Hook pulled his radio out of his pocket; it gave another electronic squawk. 'No chance of catching anything in here; we're at the limit of the range, anyway.' He went out through the front door;

he had the keys of Lambert's car, and would use the car phone if his radio would not receive.

Lambert said to Smith, 'Annoyed, was she, Mrs Pritchard?'

Everton considered the degree of her irritation. 'She shouted a bit. Told me what a useless prat I was.' He spoke without rancour, as one who had long been accustomed to more than his share of shouting.

'But she kept you on. Or did Mr Pritchard intervene on your behalf.'

Smith looked shocked. 'Oh no! She never mentioned the sack to me. By the end of the afternoon, she agreed she should really have told me about the seedlings when she set me to weeding.'

Hook appeared in the doorway, his reddish face a picture of urgency. 'We've got to go, sir.'

Lambert said to Smith, 'When are you due at The Beeches next, Everton?'

'Tomorrow afternoon.'

'Right. We'll see you there. Try to think of anything that might be connected with Mrs Pritchard's death. Anyone you saw around the place. Anything you might have heard.'

In the narrow street outside, Hook said, 'It was Chris Rushton from the station. You know Pritchard told us that his wife was going out to choir practice at the Cathedral on two evenings a week?'

'Yes. Chris was checking out to see if she had any close friends there.'

'He did that. He found that she resigned her membership over a year ago.'

Lambert whistled, almost silently. It was a situation they met often enough, most usually among philandering men. This time it was a murdered woman, in the last months of her life. 'So who was she meeting twice a week without her husband's knowledge?'

## CHAPTER EIGHT

Mark Warner found that his wife did not seem very upset about her mother's death.

He had never been sure how close mother and daughter were. In fact, he underestimated the effect of his wife's closeness to himself: Laura Pritchard's antipathy to him had coloured any affection her daughter felt towards her. Joyce Warner had never been in doubt that her loyalties lay with her husband; she had sided firmly with him in every dispute between Laura and her son-in-law.

The older woman had relaxed with her daughter in the presence of her grandchildren, but even here her love had manifested itself rather as the pride of a matriarch than that of a doting grandmother. She had rarely played with young Katie or Tim, nor could Mark remember her changing a nappy. She had read four-year-old Katie a bedtime story just once, and had never baby-sat for them. Yet in her slightly distant way Laura had seemed fond enough of the children; she had watched their play in the garden with an affectionate smile and spoken of their future with eager anticipation. Perhaps she would have been happier with older children. Now that would never be tested.

Mark had felt guilty that he should feel only a rising elation with the confirmation of Laura Pritchard's death, and had taken pains to compose himself before he went into his house to confirm to Joyce that the corpse he had been to see was indeed that of Laura Pritchard.

It seemed that he need not have worried. Joyce embraced him for a long, wordless moment when he said that the body was her mother's. Then she said quietly, 'I knew it was her. The policewoman more or less told me that it was her when she came. I'm not going to cry, Mark: I was reconciled to her death before you went there. Thank you for protecting me from that.'

And they spoke no more about it, even when the children were in bed and they sat in armchairs before a television picture which neither of them really saw. Later that night they made love, gently, with an unhurried relish of each other's bodies. It was not at all like the passionate escapism into which they had lately thrown themselves, as the Warner Plastics business fell into ever more desperate straits. This death and its discovery had brought a relaxation, not a tension, between them.

Mark woke at six to a bright summer morning, with the sun already lighting the bedroom through the thin curtains. He looked at the wife who slept beside him. During his angrier exchanges with his mother-in-law, he had sometimes revelled in the fact that Joyce looked so unlike her mother. Joyce was small and neat, with a face that was pretty but determined, framed by short, blue-black hair. She had the small features which often age quickly when the first lines appear, but he thought the cares of motherhood had in fact improved her face, giving it depth and character. Her forehead wrinkled appealingly whenever she thought hard, but in sleep it was relaxed and smooth. With her pointed chin below the straight, almost motionless mouth, she looked as innocent and as devoid of cares as a child.

Mark Warner lay for another hour and more beside her, but he did not go to sleep again. He was wondering how to ask the question which preoccupied him. It was a delicate one to put to Joyce at this stage, but much depended on the answer to it. She would know its importance as well as he did—he had never kept the details of his work from his wife, as some men did.

He need not have worried. She put the question herself over the breakfast table. 'How long do you think it will take to clear mother's will for probate?' she said.

He was at once surprised and pleased by her directness.

'I don't know, love. We can phone the solicitors and find out. Or it might be better for you to go in to the office to see them, if you feel up to it. It would be better if you did it than me, since you're going to be the beneficiary.'

Joyce's forehead puckered in the little mannerism which so delighted him; in moments of extreme perplexity, her small nose wrinkled a little in sympathy as she pushed out her top lip as an aid to thought, and he found the effect as gratifying as he had done for the last twelve years. 'I'll go in and see them this morning, when Katie's at play school. I'll take Tim in with me—that should ensure that I'm not kept waiting very long!'

Mark found himself slightly disturbed that she should show so little emotion about her dead mother. At first it had been a relief, but he was a conventional man, and he was beginning to feel that propriety demanded some manifestation of grief from a daughter. Was she putting on a brave front for him? Would she collapse into tears when he had gone off to work?

She said, 'I'll have to ring Jim Pritchard, if he doesn't contact me. He must be back from his golfing holiday by now.' She had never got used to calling her mother's second husband by anything other than his name. 'We'll need to discuss funeral arrangements, I suppose.'

Mark said awkwardly, 'There'll have to be an inquest, I imagine. But you may not need to appear, as it will be me who has to give evidence of identification.'

For the first time that morning, she looked ruffled. 'I hadn't thought of that. I suppose they'll need to establish whether it was suicide or accidental death. Did the police give you any idea what they thought about that?'

Her eyes were wide, the near-black pupils sparkling in the bright morning light of the east-facing room. It was the first time he realized how little she perhaps knew of the details of her mother's death—they had not even discussed it on the previous night. Could she really know so little? Suddenly, he wanted to protect her, but he could see no way to wrap up the harsh fact. 'I'm afraid the police believe your mother was murdered, Joyce.' The very word seemed brutal, but he could think of no way of avoiding it.

She did not seem shocked as she nodded her understanding. 'The police didn't tell me that when they came to say she was dead. I suppose they wanted to protect me.' She smiled a little at the thought, as though she was immensely experienced in the ways of the world. Mark found her expression disturbing, though he could not have said why.

She said, 'I suppose I should have expected them to say, "*Foul play is not suspected*" if they had not thought that someone had killed her. That's what they say, isn't it?'

'I think so, yes.' He was surprised anew at her composure. Perhaps it was merely a manifestation of shock. She seemed much more in control of the situation than he was, when he had expected to be providing support and consolation. He took her hands in his across the table, pausing a moment to listen to his son burbling happily in the other part of the L-shaped room. 'Would you like me to stay with you this morning? I can ring in and tell them to—'

'No, you must go in. Of course you must.'

Her earnest face seemed suddenly anxious that he should leave her. Perhaps, if she was being brave, she needed to be alone with her grief. He said, 'All right, if you're sure,' hoping that he did not sound too eager. In truth, he could not wait to get to work, to begin to ease the business out of the straitjacket which debt had imposed upon it over the last few awful months. He was already fantasizing about the interview he would have with Cummins at the bank, when the funds released by Laura Pritchard's death became available to him.

He had the BMW out of the garage and was away within five minutes. His wife watched him affectionately as he went, amused by his guilt at his desire to be away and making things happen. It was his enthusiasm for his work which was one of his most attractive qualities to her, but he never seemed to realize that.

She did not cry, as Mark had thought she might. She dressed Katie and Tim, and delivered her daughter to play school. Once she was back in the house, she rang the solicitor, as she had promised her husband she would, and made an appointment for that afternoon.

It was the middle of the morning when the phone call she had been waiting for came. When the caller announced himself, Joyce wasted no time on preliminaries. She said, 'She's been found. After she'd been in the river for a week and more. The police were round here yesterday. They got Mark to identify her, not me.'

The voice on the other end of the line said, 'That must have been a relief for you.' She tried unsuccessfully to detect whether there was an irony beneath the words; the tone was even, flat, scarcely interested.

She said, 'She was—damaged, apparently. With being in the water for so long. The police seem to be convinced it's murder. Have they managed to contact you?'

'No. Not so far.'

'You must keep away from here.'

'All right. The police will come to see you, you know. Now that they've established it's murder, you're bound to be a suspect.' The voice was as emotionless as ever—as if matricide was of no more consequence than a cracked window or a broken bottle. She was used to that in him, though. Love made you make all sorts of allowances.

Catching the note of her caller, she said evenly, 'I shall be ready for them.'

She put the receiver down and stared at it for a moment. A small smile crept on to her face, whether of amusement or affection it was impossible to tell. Perhaps it was a combination of the two.

When Mark Warner went into his office, he caught his secretary hastily thrusting a newspaper into her bag. The news of Laura Pritchard's death was already public. The sub-editors would not risk the word 'murder' until after the inquest, but they did wonders with adjectives like 'mysterious' and 'brutal', and Laura Pritchard's position as a successful businesswoman ensured that she made the headlines in death as she never had in life. A whiff of money about a violent death was the next best thing to a whiff of sex; presently, the copy suggested subtly, there might be both involved in this one.

The order from Collinsons had finally been confirmed: it seemed an omen of the happier times which lay ahead for Warner Plastics. He busied himself with calculations of the difference his mother-in-law's money would make when it released them from debt and the crippling interest rates which had so nearly brought the business down.

Joe Brown came in to see Mark about work schedules, his rolling gait proclaiming that he still saw himself as senior foreman rather than director. Mark said they no longer needed to consider laying people off. He made no attempt to discuss the buoyancy which he knew was evident this morning in his every move. He hoped it did not strike his work force as unseemly in the face of his bereavement. No doubt they would be too glad of any signs of optimism in the boss to be critical.

He put off his phone call to the bank, postponing the pleasure like a man refusing a drink until he had earned it. It was coffee-time before he asked his secretary to put him through to the manager. He found the breezy tone he wanted came to him without much effort. 'I thought I should keep you in the picture, Mr Cummins,' he said, calling up a phrase the banker had used to him in the past. 'It's about that infusion of capital which you refused me yesterday. It looks as if I shall shortly be able to secure it from another source.'

Cummins said he was happy to hear it. He did not sound at all happy.

Mark said, 'I'm just ringing to let you know that we shall

be clearing the bulk of our debts in the near future. I shall be in to see you when I know the details and can make the time. We're very busy here at the moment.'

Cummins congratulated him anaemically and said that of course he would be happy to see him whenever it was convenient. His puzzlement came down the line; perhaps he had not seen the papers, or did not know the relationship of Laura Pritchard with Mark Warner. Eventually, he tried to pull himself together. 'This is good news indeed. Perhaps when the economic climate permits a further stage of development for Warner Plastics, we might discuss how the bank might best provide support.'

Mark said, 'Perhaps we might, indeed. But of course I should have to remember just how anxious you were to help us yesterday.' He was not a vindictive man, but he not only permitted himself that closing barb, he also enjoyed it.

He was still savouring the moment when his secretary ushered in the two large men who seemed suddenly to fill his small, unpretentious office. One of them was tall and lean, with a good head of grizzled curly hair; the other burly, on the fringe of corpulence, with a cheerful, weather-beaten face and bright blue eyes. The tall man said, 'I'm Detective Superintendent Lambert and this is Detective Sergeant Hook. We are pursuing inquiries into the death of Laura Pritchard.'

Mark nodded and asked them to sit down. He had expected this, but he felt his pulse quicken with the arrival of these men. His voice was dry and a little unsteady as he said, 'I identified the body yesterday. It was—well, not very easy. But it was Mrs Pritchard.'

Lambert nodded. 'Yes. Mrs Pritchard's dentist confirmed that very promptly from his records. We like to be absolutely sure, in cases like this. That isn't meant to throw any doubt on your integrity, of course.' He looked at Warner directly and without embarrassment. 'I have to tell you that this is now a murder inquiry.'

'May I ask why you are so certain of that?' Mark managed a nervous smile.

'Mrs Pritchard had been dead for some time before she entered the water. She was strangled, with some kind of ligature. She was almost certainly attacked from behind by her killer, with a piece of rope or wire.' Lambert's tone was unemotional as he threw out the details. In a murder investigation, there was little room to protect the sensitivities of relatives who were also suspects. Their reactions to the details of murder were often interesting, as they were in this case.

Warner's blue eyes widened, and he sat down abruptly in the chair on the other side of his desk. He seemed taken aback that they should already know so much; whether he was dismayed that they should do so was not apparent. He was certainly surprised that they should reveal their knowledge so readily to him. 'Have you any—any idea who did this?'

Lambert smiled. 'You will understand that I could not reveal that to you, even if we did. But no, at the moment, we have no definite suspect for this killing. What we have to do is to build up the fullest possible picture of the victim. And of her relationships with those around her. That is why we are here, Mr Warner.' Delivering the routine statement in a monotone, he yet contrived to make it sound menacing.

Mark said, 'I won't be able to help you much there, I'm afraid. Mrs Pritchard and I were not close.' The words came easily enough; he wondered after he had delivered them if they made him sound heartless, or even guilty. These two men were used to such issues; they suddenly seemed to him to be at a tremendous advantage.

Lambert said, 'Mrs Pritchard's disappearance was not reported to us by the family. That is not unprecedented, but it is unusual.'

The superintendent's tone was carefully neutral and Warner did not take the comment as a criticism. He nodded and said, 'Her husband was away, of course, so he would not even know that she was missing. Joyce would have expected to be in contact with her mother by phone, but we wouldn't see anything particularly significant if we couldn't get through. Who was it reported her as missing?'

Hook looked at his notes. 'A Miss Hendry, who worked for your mother-in-law in Worcester. That was on Tuesday of last week.'

Warner nodded. 'I suppose she realized something was wrong when Laura didn't go in to work. We didn't have any arrangements to meet her, you see, so we didn't realize she was missing until the police asked us on Tuesday night if we knew anything about her movements.'

They checked when he had last seen Laura Pritchard. It had been with his wife, he said, on the Wednesday before her disappearance, three days before Jim Pritchard had left for his golfing holiday in Spain. That Saturday seemed so far to be the last time when she had been known to be alive. Lambert did most of the talking, with his eyes constantly on the man he questioned; that steady grey stare began to seem to Warner like an examination in itself. The other one—Sergeant Hook was it?—was noting his answers in a round, surprisingly swift hand in his black notebook.

It was Hook who now looked up and said, 'And you haven't been to the The Beeches since then?'

'No. I wouldn't have gone there on my own.'

Mark had rehearsed all this. It should have been straightforward, but he was perturbed to note how rapidly his heart beat as he gave his replies. They asked him if he knew of anyone who might have wished to harm Laura Pritchard, and he pretended to consider the matter carefully before he shook his head. 'No, not that I know of. She was a forceful woman, who did not trouble to conceal her opinions, but I don't know of any real enemies. She had her own business, of course, and I have no knowledge of that or the people who worked with her. And she had her hobbies, like the choir—I suppose there will be another circle of acquaintances there.'

Lambert nodded. There was no reason to tell this man that she had not been near the choir for a year and more. He said, 'What would you say was your own relationship with Laura Pritchard, Mr Warner?'

Mark had not prepared himself for such directness; now he realized that he should have done. 'I—we—er, weren't close.'

Hook looked up from his notes and said: 'Could you be rather more specific, sir? Had you merely a certain reserve with each other? Or were you open enemies?'

Mark wanted to minimize his differences with the dead woman. But he was no fool; he knew that these men—and other policemen—would be talking to many people who would no doubt be quite frank about himself and Laura Pritchard. 'We weren't sworn enemies, but we didn't like each other. Perhaps she never forgave me for taking away her daughter. She didn't like me as a suitor, and things got worse rather than better after I married Joyce. She appeared to think I should have gone off to work with a big company rather than starting my own one after I had left university. I don't know why; perhaps that was just an excuse for a dislike she felt anyway.'

Lambert said, 'Thank you for being frank. It's much the best way, but we waste a lot of time when people don't accept that. Was there any particular occasion of enmity in the last year or so?'

Mark had no illusions now; despite the careful phrases, the scrupulously polite tones, the acknowledgement of his cooperation, these men were going to be thorough. If they didn't get what they wanted from him or others, they would no doubt be back. He took his time, laying his hands on the desk in front of him as deliberately as if he were setting them out for inspection. But it was he, not the CID men, who examined them, as if he might find in them an aid to thought and words.

He said deliberately, 'You may as well know that my mother-in-law's death comes as a great relief to me. And to the people who work here, though they may not realize it.' Only when he had delivered the sentiment did he realize its impropriety. 'I'm speaking in purely financial terms, you understand. Warner Plastics has been in financial difficulties for some time. It's a good business, producing excellent products, but no small firms who depend upon bigger ones are proof against this recession.'

Hook said, 'You're telling us that Mrs Pritchard will have left you money in her will?'

'Not me, my wife. But it amounts to the same thing. Joyce cares as much about the business as I do.' He smiled suddenly at that thought, his delight in this conjugal closeness taking him as much by surprise as his listeners.

Hook responded with a smile of his own. 'You realize that you have just defined a motive for murder?'

Mark was unruffled. Perhaps he was even glad that someone had enunciated the thought. 'You would have found out easily enough when you spoke to other people. Joyce would have told you, for one.'

Lambert said, 'Did you ask Mrs Pritchard for financial help when she was alive?'

Warner's face clouded. He sighed; it would be better to tell them. 'Yes, I told her a few months ago about our difficulties. I asked her directly for financial assistance.' He wondered if they understood what savagely dented pride was concealed beneath those bland phrases.

'And she turned you down?'

'She turned me down flat. I rather think she enjoyed doing it. And when Joyce asked her a month later, she got the same response.' They might as well know all of it. He was struck anew by the irony that it was to be Laura Pritchard's money which would now save Warner Plastics, when in life she had been so resolutely opposed to much more modest assistance.

It was Hook who brought him abruptly back to earth,

switching the questioning again in a manner which Mark was beginning to find disconcerting. 'You seem very convinced that this money will be available. Mrs Pritchard had a husband. Is it not possible that the bulk of her estate will go to him?'

Mark ran both hands through his fair hair. As far as he was aware, it was the first involuntary gesture he had made. He thought it was excitement rather than fear which had made it happen, but it was a warning not to be overconfident. 'Jim Pritchard was her second husband, with a successful business of his own. I don't know what arrangements the two of them made, how much they discussed this. But Joyce was shown her mother's will. It leaves Laura Pritchard's share in The Beeches to her husband, and virtually everything else to her two children.'

Lambert said, 'Thank you for that information.' He made it sound as if Mark had just incriminated himself. 'Do you have an address where we can contact Mrs Warner's brother? He has so far proved rather elusive.'

Mark was relieved to have the attention diverted from him. 'No. He's in London somewhere.' As if he realized how unhelpful that was, he said apologetically, 'He's been an enigmatic character for years now. For most of the time I've known Joyce, in fact. I hardly know him, I'm afraid.'

Lambert said, 'We shall catch up with him very soon. Do you think he might have killed his mother?'

The abruptness of it made Mark catch his breath. He had to swallow before he could reply. 'No. He hasn't been around here for a long time. Why should he want to kill her?'

Lambert smiled at such naïvety. 'You have just told us that he stood to inherit a substantial sum of money. It's the oldest motive of all, and probably still the commonest.' The fact that it was a motive which also embraced the man on the other side of the desk gave him only satisfaction.

'Peter wouldn't have killed for money. He's a bit of a

drop-out, from all I hear. I'm afraid he's rather a shadowy figure, even to his sister, nowadays.'

And certainly to us, thought Lambert with irritation. 'Did Mrs Pritchard see any more of her son than his sister did?'

Mark pursed his lips, miming serious attention to the question. 'I don't think so. She could have gone up to London easily enough without our knowledge, I suppose. She didn't speak of him, but then she wouldn't have to me. She never admitted failure, and she must have seen him as one.'

Lambert was reflecting how much more difficult it was to pin down independent, intelligent women like Laura Pritchard than their unemancipated counterparts of previous generations. He said, 'What can you tell us of Mrs Pritchard's relationship with her husband?'

Mark shrugged. 'Not a lot. You'll need to ask him about that yourself, Superintendent.'

'We have done already. And we shall be back to see him again. I'm looking for someone else's view on the relationship. Just as I shall no doubt be asking other people about you, I'm afraid, Mr Warner. It's inevitable, when we are investigating a brutal and almost certainly premeditated murder.'

Mark tried not to look put out. 'Jim Pritchard was amiable enough to us. Laura was usually with him when we saw him. He was a bit—well, inhibited, I suppose you'd say—by her presence. We never really got to know him very well; remember he was only married to Laura four years ago, and we've been busy with young children for most of that time. He was always polite to Joyce, but reserved about it. As if he was watching his wife's reaction whenever he showed affection. He was pretty much the same with our children: he's never regarded them as his grandchildren.'

'But what about his relationship with his wife?'

Mark considered, then allowed himself a rueful smile.

'You must remember that I'm not an unbiased witness where Laura is concerned. But she always seemed to be the one in control. Jim is a successful businessman, and on the rare occasions when I've seen him on his own, he seems as if he would be good company, in a bluff, man's man sort of way. He spends a lot of time at his golf club, and I can see him being perfectly relaxed there.' He seized on that thought. 'Relaxed is the word. I suppose I never saw him as being properly at ease with Laura. He always seemed to be trying to present himself in a way she might approve.'

Lambert nodded. It was a different impression from the one Pritchard had given them when they saw him at the airport, but none the less valid or valuable for that. 'Do you think James Pritchard could be a violent man?'

Mark paused. He was well aware of the implications his answer would carry. 'Possibly. Given enough pressure, most of us can be violent. That doesn't mean I see him as the killer of his wife. Anyway, he was away at the time, wasn't he?'

It was Lambert's turn to pause, though his grey eyes never left the blue ones on the other side of the desk. 'It appears so, at the moment. But you yourself spoke about the state of the body when it was taken from the river. You will understand that it is impossible to establish the precise time of death from the forensic evidence. We shall have to do that by other means.' His tone left no doubt that he felt they would eventually do so.

Mark felt he sounded a little desperate as he said, 'Isn't it possible that some stranger, or someone she scarcely knew, killed her? I can't see any of her family or friends killing her like that.'

'It's perfectly possible it might be an attack by a stranger, of course. When we know the exact place and time of her killing, it will be more possible to weigh that possibility.' Lambert knew even as he exuded confidence that they might never establish those things, in a case like this. 'But at present there is nothing to support such an idea. There is no evidence of burglary, no violence upon her person except for the ligature marks, no sign of a sexual assault. We need more evidence, admittedly, but that which we have supports a view that she was murdered by someone she knew, who had planned the crime in detail.'

There was in truth not a lot of evidence to support any view yet, as he had reminded his team only that morning when he told them to keep open minds about the matter. But it did no harm to keep the pressure upon the obvious suspects until their innocence was established. He said, 'Have you knowledge of any other facts which might have any bearing upon this case?'

'No.' Sensing the end of the interview, Mark had spoken a little too promptly.

'Do you know Everton Smith?'

'No. Who is he?'

'A young man who did gardening for the Pritchards at The Beeches.'

'No. I remember they were glad to get someone reliable to work in the garden, that's all.'

Lambert stood up. 'No doubt we shall be back to see you again in due course, Mr Warner. I don't suppose you will be going away, but you shouldn't leave the area without giving us an address. For the moment, we'll say good morning to you.'

Then they were gone, for all the world as if they had been normal visitors. Mark Warner was left sitting at his desk, re-running the interview carefully in his mind. He decided that it had gone at least as well as could be expected. He was more relieved than he had anticipated that it was over.

He did not think that they had detected him in his single important lie.

## CHAPTER NINE

It was the middle of the morning now. The commuters, with their strained faces and their eyes that flashed from watch to indicator board and back again, had mostly gone.

It didn't really matter what you played for them; not here in the passage far below the city that was merely the connection between the Bakerloo and the Northern lines. They never had time to listen—not even in the moments when the crowds built until they had to shuffle along, staring anxiously forward towards the source of the bottleneck, resolutely avoiding any glance at the faces closest to them. Their ears might be open, but not to music. The coins which dropped into the greasy cap beside him then came from conscience, not appreciation.

Now that it was past ten, there were people who could hear what he played. There were even those who stopped for a moment to listen, as long as he pretended that he hadn't noticed them. He tucked the violin more firmly under his chin and resolved to make it sing. For two minutes, he indulged himself with Bach. He did it every hour—not always Bach; sometimes it was Beethoven or Schubert. He'd dropped Vivaldi since that concert hall busker, Nigel Kennedy, had taken it over. People might think he was imitating Kennedy, and he didn't want it to be thought that he imitated anyone—that was his one remaining bit of pride. Except perhaps Heifitz, whom his Dad had played on those old, scratchy records when he was a small boy.

No one paused to listen to the Bach. He wouldn't have stopped himself; you could hardly hear its purity, with the rumble of the trains in the distance. He went into the Londonderry Air, lingering shamelessly on the high notes in the way that his teacher at the Royal College would have so deplored. He deplored it himself, but it brought in the cash. He heard coins dropping into the cap as his bow caressed the strings and the notes soared. An Irish voice crooned softly about Danny Boy—all the punters called the tune that.

He had his eyes closed, as they always were when he concentrated upon his playing. He might otherwise have seen the uniforms before they were so near. The two men waited for him to finish his tune, then enjoyed the sudden alarm in the dark pupils of the deep-set eyes which he finally focused upon them.

He drew the back of his hand across his face, then bent automatically to pick up the cap and its contents. He funnelled the coins expertly into the fraying pocket of his long overcoat, noticing even in his haste that there were two fifty pence pieces, as well as the pesetas and lire which a humorous public always visited upon its parasites.

'All right, I'll move on!' he muttered. He didn't want the spiel about only doing their job.

They didn't react. When he stood upright again, with his violin hanging like an illegal pheasant at his side, the one nearest to him said, 'It's not that, lad, this time. Is your name Peter Brooke?'

It was a surprise. Even to the other men in the squat—the ones he regarded now as being closest to him—he was Jake, and had been Jake for the two months since he had been there. They didn't deal in surnames in the squats, where knowledge was rarely useful and could sometimes be dangerous. 'What if it is?' This aggression was a meaningless reflex. Both sides knew where the power lay in this exchange. He registered for the first time that these were not railway police but constables in the metropolitan force. He had never called them pigs, like the other people in the squat; that was another of his tiny assertions of individuality.

He looked up into their faces. They did not trouble to respond to his churlishness. They were watching him steadily, waiting for his next move. Looking into their young faces, he knew that they would quite welcome any lack of cooperation on his part. A little judicious aggression could safely be visited upon a man like him. 'My name used to be Peter Brooke, yes. A long time ago. Before— before this.' He lifted his arms a foot away from his sides, encompassing in the gesture many things, and then let them fall heavily back. The fiddle bounced gently against his thigh.

The shorter policeman watched the violin as suspiciously as if it was a weapon. He had short-cropped, ginger hair and broad shoulders beneath a square chin. Perhaps he had never seen a violin at close quarters before. The man he was watching raised it to his chin and drew the bow across the E string in a single, high note which rang on the tiled, concave ceiling above them. He almost went into a little piece he had written as a college exercise, years ago, then thought better of it just in time.

He said with a sudden hopelessness, 'My name is Peter Brooke, yes. Who is interested in that?'

The constable who was nearest to him creased his nose disgustedly. The odour Brooke gave off was unwholesome. And he could see ingrained dirt in the skin beneath his hairline. 'Never mind who's interested. You'll find out soon enough. You're coming along with us, lad.' He was several years younger than the man they were taking in, but the 'lad' came to him automatically, a simple means of asserting his superiority.

Peter Brooke—he was already thinking of himself as that again—wondered what would happen to his place in the squat if he was away for any length of time. They might wonder what had happened to Jake and his fiddle, but no one would defend the oily mattress in the corner for long against a new occupant. Territory was in fluid ownership in such places; everyone knew the rules, or the absence of them.

His guardians marched erect on each side of him as he

shambled along, emphasizing their authority and his submission by their gait. As the escalator rose towards the street, they stood with him on a single step, preventing anyone from climbing past them, so that a small queue of curious spectators had assembled behind them when they reached the top.

He had put his violin in its case before they moved. The uniformed men made no attempt to handle him, and he transferred it into his other hand as they emerged blinking into a June morning in London. He felt some further protest was necessary from him if the ritual was to be properly observed. He said, although he already knew the answer, 'You might at least give me some idea of what this is all about.'

The ginger one said, 'You're not under arrest. You're going to help the police with their inquiries.' He gazed straight ahead through the pale sunshine. They were not far from the station; with luck, they could deliver their prize and have time for a mug of tea before they went out again.

'What inquiries?'

It was the other, more aggressive policeman who said, 'Inquiries into the murder of a woman in Worcestershire. A woman we think is your mother, Peter Brooke.'

Joyce Warner was not taken by surprise by the CID visit. She had been anticipating it ever since she heard of the discovery of her mother's body. It was almost a relief to see the two tall men coming to the front door.

She offered them tea, and Lambert noticed that the tray with its three china cups and saucers and its matching tea pot had already been prepared. A cool customer, this one, composed and watchful. It was not at all the attitude one would have expected of a grieving daughter. But he was far too experienced to deduce much from that. Grief and its handmaiden shock took people in many different ways; those whom they hit hardest could sometimes seem the least affected.

As she poured the tea, the two men took in the room with the automatic scrutiny of experienced professionals. 'Pleasant, not ostentatious,' was Bert Hook's assessment. There was a good quality three-piece suite, a patio door to the rear garden, a bowl of rhododendron blooms and dark foliage in the hearth. There was a wedding photograph of Mark and Joyce Warner on top of a long bookcase; pictures of two toddlers at various stages of infancy occupied the rest of the same surface. Nowhere was there a picture of Laura Pritchard, not even one of her with her grandchildren.

For Hook, who had two boisterous boys of his own, the room was saved from being over-tidy by the evidence of children. A small dress and some even smaller trousers were drying on the radiator beneath the window. A teddy bear with one ear almost detached leered cheerfully at them round the corner of the bookcase. A soft yellow ball had escaped to safety beneath the television set in the corner of the room.

Perhaps Joyce Warner had noticed the survey they thought so discreet. 'You're lucky to have the place so quiet. Tim's in bed: he still has a sleep during the day,' she said. 'I haven't been in long; I've been to see the solicitor.' She had decided that there was no point in being mealy-mouthed in this interview. There was more chance of concealing what it was necessary to hide if you were frank about the things that carried no danger.

Lambert said, 'Colemans, yes. Your mother's solicitors. One of my officers was in there earlier, when you rang to make the appointment.' He smiled, broadcasting what he hoped was an air of police omniscience—that was always a disturbing thing for suspects to wrestle with. 'In cases where foul play is suspected, the terms of any will are one of the first things we have to check, of course.'

'Of course. Shortbread, Sergeant?' She handed the plate to Hook, as if the gesture was designed to demonstrate how steady her hand was in the face of this attack. It was a small, well-formed hand, and it seemed to symbolize the controlled neatness of the woman. 'You will have discovered by now that I am a major beneficiary of that will.' The dark eyes looked steadily at Lambert from the pale face with its frame of short, blue-black hair.

'That is only what one might expect. Did you know the terms of your mother's will before she died?'

'Oh, yes. She discussed it with me a year or so ago, when she made it.'

'Did it surprise you that she did not wish to leave more to her husband?'

'No. She had talked the matter through with him. They had bought The Beeches together, and her share in that was worth a considerable amount. Even in these depressed markets, the house must be worth over three hundred thousand.'

'And Mr Pritchard was happy with the arrangement?'

'Mum gave me the impression that he found it perfectly acceptable. I can't say that I've ever discussed it with Jim.'

'And you didn't think it in any way inequitable?'

She thought for a moment, wrinkling her forehead, pressing her straight lips into a thin curve. 'No, I don't think so. They had their separate lives and their separate fortunes when they decided to marry, and I suppose it seemed appropriate to me that the situation which applied before they met should be preserved. But then, I'm an interested party, aren't I?' She gave them a smile which was almost teasing. 'And you're asking me to consider a matter to which I hadn't given much thought until yesterday. There was no reason to think that Mum might not have lived for years, and changed her will, if circumstances altered.'

It was a fair point, shrewdly timed. This was a highly competent woman, who could turn out to be a formidable opponent. Lambert said, 'Do you like your stepfather, Mrs Warner?'

If he had hoped to catch her off guard by the sudden

directness, he was disappointed. She gave the question the same serious consideration she had given his previous ones, and said, 'I quite like him, yes. We have never had any kind of quarrel, and he has been—well, considerate about the situation at Warner Plastics.'

It was the first time her concern with her husband's business fortunes had been mentioned. As with her mention of the solicitor, she had led the conversation there herself rather than waiting for her interrogators to raise the matter.

Lambert said, 'Did Mr Pritchard offer any financial help?'

Joyce allowed herself a wide smile at the innocence of such a query. 'No. It would have been more than his life was worth, living with Mum. I'm sure Mark has told you about her attitude to him. Anyone who helped Mark out would have had her to contend with.'

'And her wrath would have been formidable? Forgive me, Mrs Warner, but the question is relevant: we have to build up the fullest possible picture of the victim in a murder inquiry.'

Joyce nodded, brushing away his disclaimer with a tiny gesture of her hand. 'She would have been very angry with anyone who had offered to help Mark. I shouldn't have liked to be in Jim's position if he'd tried.' She grinned, perhaps in affectionate recall of her mother's formidable personality, perhaps at the thought of her stepfather's discomfiture.

'Are you aware of any serious disagreement between the two of them?'

'Anything which would have led him to kill her, you mean?' Her calmness was becoming disconcerting, especially to Bert Hook, as he strove to record her answers. Ladies who made such good shortbread should not have the coolness appropriate to a murderer.

But she seemed only anxious to clarify the issues, so that she could give full consideration to her replies. 'No. They had different working lives, and different hobbies. For what it's worth, Mark and I thought we detected a cooling in their relationship over the last year or so. No more than that. Neither of them mentioned any difficulties in their marriage to us.'

'Would you have expected them to confide in you, if there were?'

Again, her small, regular features were lit for a moment by that disarming, unembarrassed smile. 'A fair point. Jim Pritchard certainly wouldn't have talked about such things to us. And we hardly ever saw him without Mum being with him, anyway. My mother might have said something to me when we were alone together, but I think she'd have had to be desperate. She knew that I don't keep secrets from Mark, and she certainly wouldn't have wanted him to know about any personal difficulties she had.'

She was taking every opportunity to emphasize how close a marriage she enjoyed, as her husband had earlier. Not for the first time, Lambert wondered if more than one person had been involved in this crime—when a body had to be transported, two people made things much easier. He said, 'So you don't think Mr Pritchard was involved in any way in the murder of his wife?'

Again she gave them that wry, slightly ironic smile: it was almost a mannerism now. 'He was away, wasn't he? Anyway, for what it's worth, I don't think Jim has it in him to be a murderer.'

It was Lambert who smiled now: he had heard that confident opinion expressed too often to take much account of it. He said, 'When did you last see your mother, Mrs Warner?'

She had her answer ready. Again, she delivered it with no obvious sign of distress. 'It was on the Thursday before she died. Two days before Jim went off on his golfing holiday. I went over to The Beeches on that afternoon. We had tea together, in the conservatory at the back of the house. I was there for about an hour.'

'Thank you for being so precise.' He was carefully neutral, lest she should suspect a criticism.

She said only, 'I knew you would want to know, so I thought about it before you came.'

Perhaps Lambert was a little nettled by her equanimity. He said abruptly, 'Where is your brother, Mrs Warner?'

This time the sudden switch of tack did rattle her. Her face flushed before she said, 'Peter had nothing to do with this. Why are you even asking about him?'

'He is a main beneficiary of the will, as you are. Until we can speak to him, we shall certainly be interested in him. The more elusive he is, the more interested we shall become. We may in due course be able to eliminate him from the inquiry, but only if we can talk to him and verify his movements at the time of the murder.'

He wondered if she realized how vague they still were about the exact timing of this death. The Severn had done the work the killer had planned that it should on the corpse; they could not yet be certain about the day of the death, let alone the hour. Perhaps the house-to-house investigative team would throw up some sightings of the victim, and even of those who had been near to her when she died.

Her brow was wrinkled again in that oddly attractive accompaniment to her thoughts. 'Peter's in London. He isn't on the phone there.'

'But you have an address?'

'No. He—he moves about.'

Lambert had heard on his way here that a man thought to be Peter Brooke had been brought into a station in London. He would keep that news to himself, unless he found a moment where it might be useful here. 'But he is in touch with you.'

He had made it a statement, and she accepted it as such. 'Not regularly. He rings me up from time to time.'

'And he comes down here. To see you and his mother.'

'From time to time, yes.'

Her reluctance gratified him: he took it as a sign of vulnerability. 'And when was the last time?'

'Oh, quite some time ago now.' Her hasty vagueness was

a contrast to her earlier precision, and he let her words hang for a moment in the air between them, until she found the evasion embarrassing. 'It must have been about a month before—before Jim Pritchard went off on holiday.'

'And what was the purpose of that visit?'

'Oh, nothing in particular. Peter tends to turn up when the mood takes him. It isn't often for any particular purpose.'

'A social visit, then. He came here?'

'Yes.'

'And he went to The Beeches?'

'No. Not that I know of. I'm sure he didn't.'

'But he saw your mother.' He made it a statement again; the sudden edginess in her manner had convinced him of the fact.

'Yes. He saw her here.' She put up a hand to check on her hair, though not a strand was out of place.

'Did he ask her for money?'

For the first time, she let her annoyance show. 'No, he did not. He didn't see her for more than twenty minutes. And he would never have asked her for money.'

'Because he did not need it, or because she would not have helped him?' Her neat, oval face had set sullenly. When she did not answer, he said, 'Was Peter on good terms with his mother, Mrs Warner?'

'Good enough, yes. He was always closer to his father.' She spoke now as if she grudged them every word.

'And his father is dead?'

'Yes.'

'Did Peter resent your mother's second marriage?'

'You'd better ask him that yourself. If you can find him.' It was the first moment of pique she had permitted herself, and she curtailed it immediately.

Lambert said, 'We will. Possibly later today.' He was already regretting his dispatch of Detective Inspector Rushton to the capital to see the brother of this cool young woman. But one could not be everywhere: that was why murder investigations were team efforts. He saw that his confidence had shocked her, and was gratified; probably she had thought it would take the police machine longer to locate her mysterious brother.

They were standing up and she was relaxing, in the impression that their meeting was over when Lambert said, 'Who do you think killed your mother, Mrs Warner?' The Chief Constable wouldn't have liked that direct approach with a grieving daughter, but he had not seen many overt signs of grief here.

Joyce Warner was neither ruffled nor offended by the question. She said, 'I've thought about it, of course. I'm sure it wouldn't be anyone in the immediate family. Mum had friends and acquaintances we don't even know; that's been especially true over the last few years. But my guess is that she was killed by someone she didn't even know herself.'

Husband and wife had offered the same proposal for a murderer. Lambert recalled Mark Warner's, 'Isn't it possible that some stranger, someone she knew scarcely or not at all herself, killed her?'

It was a very convenient hypothesis for both of them.

## CHAPTER TEN

Along roads flanked with the rich greens of early summer, the big Vauxhall moved at the sedate pace which signified that its driver was thinking.

But it was the passenger, Bert Hook, apparently immersed in a consideration of the oaks of Herefordshire, who eventually said, 'There is something odd about the Warners.'

Lambert grinned. 'But what? There's something odd about most of us, Bert. The question is whether the Warners' oddness is connected with homicide.'

'They're hiding something—both of them are, I'm sure.'

'You're probably right. But is it connected with our murder? And are they both hiding the same thing, or entirely different things?'

Bert decided that if the chief was going to be gnomic, he had better stonewall. 'We'll need to come back to them when we have more facts from elsewhere,' he said firmly.

Lambert recognized a defensive conclusion which he had often used himself. 'Yes. There is an annoying scarcity of facts in this case.' There usually was when a body was discovered so long after death, and both of them knew it. 'I spoke to Chris Rushton last night. On the information which had come in then from forensic and the house-to-house teams, we still haven't established any satisfactory time of death.'

As usual, Lambert was breaking the unwritten rules of police procedure in using his detective inspector—Rushton—to collate the mass of information pouring into the Murder Room from his team, whilst he kept in direct touch with the investigation himself. The superintendent was regarded in the force as an eccentric, a survival of an older generation, whose methods were tolerated because he got results. Results are always the best defence of any deviation from the norm in a conservative organization like the police. Even his new chief constable, George Harding, seemed prepared to accept the way Lambert operated, when many had expected him to reject it.

'When was Laura Pritchard last seen alive?' asked Hook. A younger officer might not have cared to show such ignorance of the case. Hook knew his value, and the man he was addressing also knew it. He knew too that Bert had been busy with his Open University studies in his limited spare time: 'keeping crime in perspective' as Lambert called it.

'So far, we can only put it as late as the Saturday when Jim Pritchard left for his golfing holiday,' said Lambert. 'She seems to have left a note for her cleaning lady on the Tuesday, but there is no sighting of her on that day as yet.'

'Pritchard seems to be the only one in the clear,' said Hook.

'Yes. And even that needs confirmation. He says he left her alive and well, but so far we haven't actually got statements from people who saw her after he'd left. Even the fellow golfers who went with him on the holiday don't recall seeing anything of Mrs Pritchard when they picked him up.'

'No? Wouldn't a wife normally have waved him off if she wasn't going to see him for ten days?'

'Probably. But we already have some evidence that Laura Pritchard wasn't a normal wife, if indeed there is such a creature. And they did leave very early in the morning. She might not have been up and dressed.'

'What about Everton Smith?' Hook raised the name with the air of a man who knew he must, to preserve his professional impartiality. He had a predilection towards the underdog which was the source of much amusement among his fellow CID operators. In their collective opinion, the underdog was much the most likely candidate for most crimes, and they could quote statistics to support that view.

'He's the only one so far from outside the family whom we know had contact with the victim at around the time of her death. And we know he'd had a heated argument with her a month or two earlier.' Lambert kept his gaze on the road; it was impossible to tell from his long, unmoving face whether or not he was teasing his sergeant.

Hook said doggedly, 'But there must be other people like him, people we simply haven't found yet.'

'Be interesting to know where Everton's getting his money from. His unemployment cheques haven't paid for that bike and its insurance. Not on top of his other living expenses.'

'So he's exploiting the black economy, like a million others. It doesn't make him a murderer.'

Lambert grinned. 'It might make him communicative,

though, when we put the pressure on him. I feel young Mr Smith has more to tell us yet.'

'And so, no doubt, have the people Laura Pritchard employed,' said Hook defensively.

They were on their way to see those people now. Brooke Office Services—Mrs Pritchard had obviously chosen to keep the business in her previous name—operated in Worcester. The office was some fifteen miles from her home, and perhaps the same distance from the spot where her body had been discovered in the Severn.

They had moved out of Herefordshire and into Worcestershire now. Neither of these men acknowledged the unhistorical yoking together of the two counties in the unseemly local government reclassifications of the 'sixties. As Bert Hook pointed out to anyone who would listen, the reorganization didn't even make sense in cricketing terms. He looked at the brooding escarpment of the Malvern Hills on his left, and over beyond Lambert to where the Severn could be glimpsed on the other side of the old Vauxhall.

The great river wound its way through flat country here, in a series of huge curves which glinted silver in the bright late-morning light. Hook thought of the damaged corpse which had been the starting point of this investigation, winding its slow way round those bends in the water, lodging against submerged obstructions, then resuming its grisly progress as the current or the wind freed it to move again.

'Love, lust and lolly,' said Bert reflectively, enunciating the three favourite coppers' motives; one or more of them was said to underlie every serious crime. 'We've only got lolly as a possibility in this one.'

'So far,' said Lambert cautiously. 'It's early days yet. We haven't unearthed a mistress for Jim Pritchard, which could have led him to a contract killing. We haven't found a lover for his wife, who killed her when she wouldn't break up her marriage for him—or simply when she ditched him.

All things are still possible.' He didn't look as if the thought filled him with joy.

Brooke Office Services was a compact modern enterprise in a side street near the middle of Worcester.

A notice in the window, easily legible without being garish, proclaimed the firm's ability to provide secretarial services of all kinds at twelve hours' notice. A bright, intelligent woman of about thirty met them with an interrogatory smile. There were flowers as well as phones and a computer upon her desk, and the place smelt fresh and airy.

Once they had explained the purpose of their visit, she took them past a list of vacancies to the rear of the room and a door which carried the words 'Sue Hendry, Manager'.

Ms Hendry was at first sight as crisp and efficient as the enterprise she directed. The policemen, who assessed age automatically and expertly as part of the normal process of observation, put her at about forty, though most people would have made her a little younger. She had red hair, and the sandy eyebrows beneath a square forehead argued that its shade was entirely natural. She pointedly refused to take a chair until her visitors were seated, and her firm nose and chin reinforced her determined, slightly aggressive air.

Lambert had been educated in an old-fashioned, single-sex, grammar school, with a similar girls' establishment separated only by a high fence and a few straggling trees. It was a legacy of much surreptitious observation through that fence that he could now picture Sue Hendry playing tennis or hockey in a cheerful, no-nonsense way, full of brisk energy and swirling short skirts. He banished that inappropriate image almost as quickly as it arrived.

She sat down not behind her desk but in an armchair opposite the two CID men, so that her face was no more than six feet from theirs. And they saw that the skin beneath her bright green eyes was puffed and a little red. The efficient and composed Ms Hendry had been crying. Either the prospect of talking about her employer had distressed her, or something quite unconnected with Laura Pritchard had upset her during the morning. But she did not look the kind of lady who would easily be thrown off balance by events in her working environment.

Lambert said, 'I expect Sergeant Hook here explained the purpose of our visit when he rang to make this appointment.'

'To talk about Laura's murder, yes.'

It was direct and simple. Yet it told them more than she realized it did. That she had been on first name terms with her deceased employer, for a start. That this business probably operated on the informal basis that this implied, with no exaggerated regard for the niceties of rank. And that the woman before them was not concerned to wrap up unpleasant words like 'murder' in some more anodyne packaging.

Lambert explained, as always, that their concern was to build up as full a picture as possible of the murder victim, and she nodded rather impatiently, as if anxious to dispense with the preliminaries as quickly as possible. He said, 'Can you tell us when you last saw your employer, please?'

She looked as if she had been slapped across the face. He was left wondering what could have offended her in the simple, routine question. Was it the use of the term 'employer'? Surely she could not be so thin-skinned. And the details which they had checked before they came specifically named her as a manager and not a partner in the firm.

She answered crisply enough when she spoke. 'I last saw Laura on the Friday afternoon before she died. It was here. And she left at three-thirty precisely.'

'Thank you.' She had delivered it as though she had said it all before. But no one else involved in the inquiry had questioned her. She must have listed the facts for her own satisfaction. 'How long have you worked here, Ms Hendry?'

The title still fell awkwardly from his lips, despite his resolute employment of it over the last few years.

'It's Miss.' She allowed herself a small smile at his expense. 'I've been here for three years now.'

'And you did not know Mrs Pritchard before that?'

'No.'

'Did you find her a considerate employer?'

Again she looked distressed, and this time he was sure it was by the use of that word 'employer'. He was at a loss to understand why; it seemed a neutral enough word to him. She seemed to be striving for calmness when she said, 'She was extremely considerate, yes.'

'And other people as well as you found her so?'

She flashed him a sudden look of molten dislike, then covered the emotion just as quickly. 'I think so. You'd need to ask them.'

'But at the moment I'm asking you, Miss Hendry.' He had no objection to ruffling a few feathers; irritation, like other emotions, could lead to revelations.

She seemed to be striving for something—perhaps it was objectivity. 'Laura never asked anyone to do what she could not have done herself. But she was a highly competent person, and not everyone found it easy to match her standards.'

So there had been high words in this immaculate office sometimes. And perhaps more. 'Were there sackings?'

Sue Hendry was finding this more difficult than it should have been. 'The only people we employ directly are the three in this building. One of them was replaced, about a year ago. There have been some office workers whose services have not been retained, when their work has not come up to the standards we think appropriate. You must understand that this is a business which operates very much on word of mouth recommendations. We provide people with reliable secretarial staff; in turn, they come to trust our standards.'

She sounded as if she was quoting someone else, rather

than producing these sentiments from herself. Her source could only be the late Mrs Pritchard. Lambert felt at last that he was getting a fuller picture of that formidable lady. He said, 'But you found her easy enough to work with yourself?'

She hesitated, so that for a moment he thought she was going to reveal more than he had expected. Then the green eyes flashed from him to Hook, whose head was bent dutifully over his notebook, and she said, 'Laura was excellent to work with. Once she realized that I knew what I was doing, she allowed me to use my own initiative and very rarely questioned any decision I made. We discussed things together; she even allowed me to help formulate the future policy of the firm. We went through some difficulties together, shortly after I arrived as manager, in the midst of this recession, but we survived those and our reputation is now such that even in these times business has continued to grow.'

It was informative, but again the delivery made it sound almost like an evasion. It lacked the animation it should have had, and the monotone made it sound as if she was reading out a written testimonial. She spoke as if she could scarcely believe that she was saying these things herself. Partly because he was preoccupied with her odd manner, he prolonged the discussion of Brooke Office Services, saying, 'That is a tribute to both of you. Not many businesses are expanding at present.'

She blushed, then looked embarrassed as she felt the blood rush to her cheeks. Probably, like most people with her colouring, she blushed easily. She said, 'It's easier to get good staff to work as temps nowadays, of course. A lot of efficient secretarial staff have lost their jobs in this area through no fault of their own over the last few years. We have a good list of competent staff available for temporary work now. Sorry, that sounded like a commercial.' She seemed once more the professional, capable woman.

Lambert wondered why she had been so natural in this

explanation, and so rigid in her previous one. The reason could only lie in her relationship with the dead woman, which was decidedly interesting. Perhaps he might find out more about Laura Pritchard here than he had done so far from her family. He said, 'How often was Mrs Pritchard here? We understand that she no longer worked full time in the business.'

'No. Since she found that she could let go of the reins without the coach going off course, she felt less need to be here at all times. Over the last two years, she has gradually left more and more of the day-to-day running of things in my hands.' She found it impossible to keep the pride out of her voice as she said it.

'It must have been gratifying to find yourself trusted by someone with her high standards.'

He had intended it as no more than an emollient sentence to keep her talking, in the hope of eliciting more detail. But he found that she was blushing again, with an embarrassed, almost girlish pleasure. She clasped her small, perfect hands in her lap as she said almost eagerly, 'It did, frankly. Laura didn't suffer fools gladly. But she was also shrewd and perceptive; when I found that we were operating as equals in developing the firm, it gave me quite a kick.'

She sat upright and put her hands now on the arms of her chair. With her earnest, open face, her firm bust showing to advantage beneath the cotton sweater, her clear nail varnish accentuating the faultless fingers, she had the slightly aggressive air of a sixth-former determined to assert her rights. Like many people who have had no previous dealings with the law, she had found herself feeling vulnerable, even in her own environment. It was Hook, speaking for the first time, who reminded her that she had still not been precise in recalling her employer's working week. 'So exactly how much time did Mrs Pritchard spend here?'

It was a simple enough question, but she looked at him as if he was trying to trap her. It was a few seconds before she said, 'She was usually here for two full days in each week. Not necessarily the same days each week: we decided when it would be most useful for her to be here.' Suddenly, she was fumbling in the handbag she had put down beside her on the carpet. She dabbed at her eyes with a small plain handkerchief and said, 'Sorry. I thought I was going to be all right, but—' She dissolved into silent tears, unable to complete the sentence.

Lambert said, 'There's no hurry. I expect she came in for shorter periods as well as the full days.'

She nodded, grateful for his help. Eventually, she managed to say unevenly, 'She popped in on most days. She didn't always stay long, if we weren't busy enough to need her efforts.'

Lambert remembered reading somewhere that writers should have a splinter of ice in their hearts, so that they could record things objectively when those around them were overcome by emotion. He had reflected that that splinter of ice was even more necessary for detectives. He knew that he had it, and sometimes despised himself in retrospect for the ruthlessness he showed in the face of grief. Now he watched the woman suffering before him and decided coolly that if he gave a little, he might get back more information from this employee than he had done from Laura Pritchard's husband and daughter.

He said, 'We have to learn everything we can about Mrs Pritchard, in the hope that the knowledge will suggest pointers to the way she might have died. In particular, we need all the detail we can find about her movements in the week or ten days before she died.'

Sue Hendry nodded seriously, as if forcing all her concentration into the understanding of his words. Her tearful and distressed face showed all of her forty years now, but her reactions and movements provided a strange contrast: they had the elaborate care of a very serious child. Suffering and shock strip us all bare of the pretences we adopt to shield us from the world around us, thought Lambert. He had seen similar effects to this often in those left behind after violent death.

Callously, he wondered why this woman, who was not a relative but an employee, should be so affected. He said, 'It was you who first reported Mrs Pritchard's disappearance to us.'

'Yes. She hadn't come in to work, and hadn't phoned in to say that she was ill. That was quite out of character; she was always so—so reliable.' She faltered as she searched for that word, then recovered determinedly to say, 'I knew then that there must be something seriously wrong, you see.'

Lambert wondered if she knew how unusual it was for the report of a missing person to come from workplace rather than family. He said, 'It appears that Mrs Pritchard had her secrets. As you would expect, we are bound to be interested in those during a murder inquiry.'

Her only response was to stare steadily down at the floor between them, convincing him that she knew something he had not so far discovered about the murder victim. He decided to feed her something more specific. 'We know that Mrs Pritchard was a member of the Cathedral Choir at Hereford,' he said. She looked up at him for a moment, then nodded sharply and dropped her gaze back to the floor. He said quietly, 'But we know that for the last year and more, she has not been attending rehearsals, when her family thought that she was doing so.'

Again the little nod of understanding, this time without looking up at him. He gave her time, but she said nothing, so he went a little further. 'The most usual explanation when people go in for deceptions of this kind is that they are meeting a lover.' The head opposite him gave an even smaller, almost imperceptible nod. She lifted the little ball of wet handkerchief again and gave a little dab at each eye.

Lambert said, 'I think you agree with that, Miss Hendry. And I think you know who that lover was.'

She looked up at him and held his gaze at last. The

green, tear-washed eyes were clear and defiant. 'Of course I do. If you were as sharp as you're supposed to be you'd have spotted it by now. Laura and I were lovers, for the last two years of her life.'

Now at last her grief was audible. Her sobs rang loud in the small room, and neither of the awkward men could find anything with which to comfort her.

## CHAPTER ELEVEN

There was brisk activity at Warner Plastics. The owner's new-found air of optimism had run through the close-knit work force. No one now thought the firm was heading for extinction; no one looked anxiously at the tiny column of situations vacant in the local press.

As if the spirit was spreading out to customers too, there was confirmation of another order, and a couple of promising inquiries which could lead to contracts in the future. Mark Warner felt so buoyed up and energetic that he had to beware of seeming positively smug to those who had seen him so cast down only two days ago. He wondered if his voice rang a little too loud from his office; was conscious that he laughed openly several times as he moved among the men at their machines—that was a sound which they had not heard from him in months.

Yet at the back of his mind there crawled a tiny worm of disquiet. All was not yet concluded with the death of Laura Pritchard. He had looked for something at home that morning and been unable to find it. It was a small, innocent object in itself; indeed, he could scarcely think of anything more innocent. But if it was found in the wrong place, it could lead to disaster for him. And he was not even certain where it lay.

At eleven-thirty, when Lambert and Hook were beginning their revealing exchange with Sue Hendry in

Worcester, Mark Warner dialled a number he knew by heart. He did not think there would be any reply. If there was, he would simply put the phone down. If no one picked the phone up, that would surely mean the place was empty. That would give him the chance to search it. He would have to take the risk of being disturbed.

He let the phone ring fifteen times, imagining it echoing round the empty room. There was no reply.

Three minutes later, he told his secretary he would be away until after lunch and hurried out to the big BMW. She noticed how clear were his blue eyes, how vivid his fair colouring, how he carried with him an air of scarcely suppressed energy. Like a consumptive in the grip of that disease, she thought. Being much given to the reading of historical novels with Victorian settings, she considered herself now an expert on the symptoms of this particular affliction.

Mark felt a moment of panic as he drove swiftly away from the place where he felt in control. Driving the BMW soothed his nerves. After the first few miles, he began to feel in control of himself again. Beneath the glittering blue eyes which had so impressed his secretary, his mouth was a straight, determined line.

Peter Brooke was still getting used to his old identity. He had worked so hard at being 'Jake' in the squat that his former name sat uneasily upon him now, like a jacket which had been long forgotten in an old wardrobe.

How should Peter Brooke behave in the place in which he now found himself? It would have been easier for Jake, he thought. As far as he could remember, Peter had never been in a police station in his life. Let alone in one like this.

Police stations in central London reflect the business they conduct. In the last decade, drugs and a violent society have had their inevitable effect. Brooke was put in a cell which had white tiles from floor to ceiling, many of them cracked. The whole corridor of cells had been swabbed out that morning, but the odour of stale vomit was still faintly discernible through the stronger smell of disinfectant. He had not been asked to empty his pockets or to surrender the means of killing himself; he decided that this meant he was probably not under arrest. They had even let him keep his violin, when they saw him wrap both arms protectively around the old case.

Could he demand to be released and walk out? It was a long time since he had stirred his brain with considerations like this, and he did not feel it was reliable. He had cultivated apathy for too long for it to release him easily now. In any case, he doubted that he could summon the force of will to assert his rights, if that is what they were.

When Brooke had sat on the wooden bench for an hour, glancing up occasionally at the single white light behind its wire shield in the ceiling, an eye studied him for a moment through the hole in the door. Apparently it decided he was not dangerous, because, a few moments after the flap had been slid shut, the door was noisily unlocked and he was given a mug of sweet tea. He did not take sugar, and the tea was warm rather than hot, but he knew better than to complain. When you lived as he did now, you did not have to respect authority, but you recognized the futility of challenging it.

As he drank the tea, he studied from the corner of his eye the man who brought it to him. He was an older officer in shirtsleeves, with greying hair and the beginnings of a paunch. Peter decided that a man like this would not feel the need to assert his superiority; then he asked him what he could expect to happen next.

'VIP, aren't you, lad?' said the man. He looked Brooke up and down, as though noticing for the first time that he was more than a parcel, to be guarded and delivered in due course. 'Not to be questioned by the likes of us. Not even by our local CID. You're waiting for an inspector to come up from Oldford, you are. What you been up to?' He did not seem to expect an answer, so Peter grinned into his empty mug and said nothing. But the custody sergeant was not unfriendly. He gathered up the empty mug and promised his charge some grub if his interrogator wasn't there within the hour.

It was another two hours before Detective Inspector Christopher Rushton was ready to see him. They met in a stifling interview room, so small that its green walls were scored and pitted near the floor with the marks of chairs moved too hastily back. They sat on upright chairs at either side of a table no more than two feet square, where they could study each facial spasm, each change of inflection in speech.

They could smell each other, too. Brooke caught the sharp scent of aftershave from the inspector; Rushton had not been in the room for a minute before he caught the stale body-scent of a man who had not troubled over-much about washing in the preceding weeks. The one thing they could not do was to touch each other, despite their proximity; any hint of violence on either side would be instantly checked.

Rushton set the tape running, announcing the interview and the time of its commencement. He said, 'You are helping us with our inquiries into the death of Laura Pritchard, which took place some ten to fourteen days ago in suspicious circumstances. Was the lady your mother?'

Brooke, who had had three hours since the police had brought him in from the underground station to consider his tactics, had decided that this had better be as straightforward as he could make it. 'Yes. She used to be Mrs Brooke, you see, before she became Pritchard.'

'And when did you last see her, Mr Brooke?' Rushton always liked to get the title in at least once at the beginning of an interview: you never knew who might be listening to the tape in due course.

'About six weeks ago, I think.' That was what they had agreed; Peter tried to deliver the phrase with confidence.

He had been given a plate of surprisingly appetising stew

while he waited. But he was not used to eating in the middle of the day, and perhaps he had eaten a little too eagerly in that depressing cell. He found he now had indigestion, and he wished this cool man in the sharp suit would not watch him quite so closely. In the squat, they came and went for days at a time without ever looking each other full in the face.

'Did she come to see you in London?'

He smiled at the absurdity of the idea, surprising himself. The picture of his mother in the squat, with her immaculately cut clothes and carefully coiffured hair, was vividly comic to him. He put his hands on the table in front of him, noticing for the first time in days how black his nails were, thinking how distressed his mother would have been at the sight of them. He had cut them—you could not play the fiddle with your nails too long. But washing was not easy in the squat. They still had water, but the electricity had been cut off, so that they only had the cold tap, and you had to queue for that. Sometimes it didn't seem worth queuing for it; he realized now that those times had come more often recently.

He said carefully, 'My mother never came to see me in London. I don't see her very often these days. When I do, it's back in Herefordshire.' He enunciated the name carefully, like a man who is proud of his geography. The effect was ruined by a little hiccup of wind from his indigestion: it made him sound disconcertingly like a drunk.

Rushton noted the use of the present tense, but registered it as normal. It wasn't unusual: it took time for bereaved relatives to come to terms with death, especially when it was sudden. He said, 'It took us some time to find you, Mr Brooke: no one seemed to have an address for you. How did you find out about your mother's death?'

Brooke recognized the first real danger. He tried to sound calm and matter-of-fact as he said, 'I ring my sister from time to time. Joyce Warner, of Avonlea, 24 Pangbourne Lane, Woolnorth, Gloucestershire.' He reeled off the address, finding it helped to still the racing he felt in his mind. He was disappointed that he could not remember the postcode to finish it off.

'We have already seen Mrs Warner. She told us about you.' It was Rushton's first phrase of aggression. Lambert had thought the detective inspector would be too cold and hostile, too inflexible, to get all they wanted from a man who was by all accounts a drop-out. In fact, Rushton, immaculately clean, smartly dressed, already well up the ladder of his chosen profession, felt a curious affinity with the strange figure who sat across the table from him.

The one element they had in common was loneliness. But it was so powerful a bond that it seemed for a while more important to Rushton than all the myriad differences of the two who were set as opponents in that tiny, stifling room. Rushton's wife had left him. It was so common a happening in the police force that after the first few days it scarcely excited comment. There was understanding, even sympathy, but also an unspoken view among Chris Rushton's colleagues that such things were only to be expected.

Yet each tragedy is an individual one, each sterility in a man's life diminishes him in a different way. Rushton had grown used to the police system, to operating by the rule book; he had found that his temperament even enabled him to enjoy the order which that book brought to his life. The discovery that his personal life had no book of rules, that his wife acknowledged no duty to the force and its code, had not only taken him by surprise but left him with no defence. Her departure, and that of his infant daughter, had hit him hard—much harder than he could acknowledge to his colleagues. He was too proud for that. He could not even accept their sympathy; he cut it off at source.

But in the dark hours, while he lay awake in his silent house, Detective Inspector Rushton, whizz-kid of the CID and efficient bureaucrat of the Incident Room, had wept the tears about which his colleagues must never know.

Now he saw in the man opposite him the desolation he

could never acknowledge in himself. Peter Brooke had that unkemptness about his cheeks which was neither a beard nor the 'designer stubble' which a few mistaken sports personalities and pop stars had made fashionable. He simply had not shaved for several days; on the last occasion he had done so, he had either used a very blunt blade or been in no state to control his hand, for the growth on his face was uneven and there were small scars upon his chin and upper lip, visible from a few feet away.

As he sat at the table, his shoulders were hunched like those of a much older man—an old lag, thought Rushton suddenly, though there was no criminal record of even minor offences against this man. His cuffs were not just frayed but ragged too; the collar points of his unironed shirt curled upwards around his thin neck; where the open neck exposed his throat, it was pitted with the grime of days spent busking in the hot depths of the London Underground.

But it was in his dark eyes, so deep-set that they accentuated his furtive air, that Rushton thought he saw the isolation of this man and found an unlikely fellow-sufferer. This man manifested his loneliness in self-neglect, whereas Rushton had become even more careful of his appearance, almost dapper in his masking of the anguish he could not show. Nevertheless, he felt now the bonding of a desolation which was common to both of them. For a moment, for the first time since his wife had left him, he found himself wanting to talk about his own truncated life, to reveal himself as a counterpart to the man across the table who sat waiting for him to attack.

He did not do any such thing, of course. Rushton was a natural policeman, with all the strengths and weaknesses that the calling extracts from its followers. The CID man in him saw Brooke's loneliness as an opportunity. This flotsam upon the heaving surface of city life would surely not hold out for long against the interrogation of a highly trained detective inspector. He shut out his own life and waited for his moment.

There was a considerable interval before Brooke said in a low voice, 'What did Joyce tell you about me?'

Rushton smiled at him, letting uncertainty work on the man for a moment before he responded. Behind his mask, he was thinking furiously. He would not let Brooke know that he had not seen the sister himself, that his only source of information was a hasty phone call to Lambert before he began this interview. The chief fancied this man's only close relationship might be with his sister, and the few words Peter Brooke had volunteered so far suggested that he was right. So he might want to talk about her. Rushton might let him do that in due course. But not now: he would grill him about something else—get him on the run and keep him there.

'You didn't like your mother, did you, Peter?' he said suddenly.

It was an instinctive piece of aggression, which paid immediate dividends. Brooke flashed him a look in which astonishment and fear were fused. For a moment, he was prepared to deny the allegation. Then he said, 'No, I didn't. Sometimes I hated her. She killed my father, you know.'

For a moment, Rushton thought he had found the CID man's dream, the discovery of a crime long buried and now instantly solved, a revelation of a murder which officers before him had only suspected. He kept his voice quite calm as he said, 'And how was that, Peter?'

'She walked out on him. He died within the year. They said it was cancer, and it was, of course. But he wouldn't have had it, without what she did to him. No one will ever convince me otherwise.' He produced the last phrase like an older man, set in his ways; he must have used it to reject consolation many times before.

'When was this, Peter?' Rushton's soft, sympathetic tone needed no effort; he spoke as one who had himself been abandoned.

'Seven years ago. All but three weeks.'

Precision can sometimes be more significant than evasion, thought his interrogator. 'And were you living at home then?'

'No. Except sometimes during the holidays. I expect that was why I never saw it coming.' He put his grubby hands on the table and studied the black nails with distaste, as if they belonged to some other and more squalid man. He was back for a moment in a happier time, when the world had seemed to lie before him and his nails had never been dirty.

'You were in college at that time?'

'At the Royal College of Music, yes. In my third year.' Rushton's glance strayed automatically to the battered violin case he had brought into the room with him, shielding it as tenderly as if it had been an old dog. Brooke, intercepting that look, said, 'I never completed the course. Dad got ill, you see, after she'd left. Took it hard, he did, her going like that.' For a moment, the Gloucestershire accent came riding on emotion through his educated speech. Rushton knew in that moment that Brooke senior had not had much schooling, that the lapse was an unconscious tribute to his memory.

Rushton, coming from Cheltenham himself, found himself dropping responsively into the accent as he said, 'You miss your dad still, don't you, Peter?'

Brooke nodded, looking very tired suddenly. 'He was the one who got me into music, see? He couldn't play himself, but he listened all the time. He took me to concerts while I was still a nipper. Worked overtime at the shop to get me lessons. He wanted to live to see me in a symphony orchestra, but he didn't quite make it.' The tragedy was etched in the premature lines of the young face.

Automatically, the DI in Rushton noted this vulnerability, then sought to exploit it. 'But you were never as close to your mother?'

'No. Not even before she left.'

'And once she had done that, things were never patched up, were they? They went from bad to worse.'

Brooke seemed to accept that his questioner knew all about this, whereas in reality Rushton was groping in the dark, playing by instinct in a way that might have surprised his chief. The young man stared at the table as he said harshly, 'She couldn't even weep at his funeral. She only left her office for an hour. I suppose she had another man by then.' He paused, looked again at his hands, this time unseeingly, and said, 'I hated her. I'm glad she's dead.'

It was the second time he had spoken of his hate. Rushton reflected that this was hardly the tactic of a man out to conceal his guilt. He said, 'That shouldn't prevent you from helping us to find out who killed her, Peter. Murder is the worst of crimes, whoever the victim.' He felt like a clergyman instructing a candidate for Confirmation. This man could not be very much younger than he was himself, but his air of abstracted innocence made him seem an adolescent. Rushton had seen the same demeanour once before: that man, who had killed his wife and child, was now in Broadmoor.

Brooke said wearily, 'What do you want me to tell you?'

'What do you know of your mother's second husband, James Pritchard?'

'Nothing. I've only seen him once. I didn't go to the wedding, and I've never wanted to know him.' His lips were set in a sullen line.

'How much older than you is your sister?'

'Four years.' The dark eyes were studying him now from within their deep sockets, pondering what traps were being set for him by these sudden shifts of questioning.

'And what did she think of her mother?'

'Not a lot.' Rushton said nothing, and eventually the man seemed to realize the inadequacy of his childish response. 'She kept closer to Mother than me, after she left our dad. Tried to bring us back together, sometimes, but I wasn't having that.'

'Do you think Joyce might have killed Laura Pritchard?'

His hands gripped the table, so that the dirt stood out even more clearly against the white of bone beneath it. 'Of course not. Joyce might not have liked her, but she wouldn't kill anyone.'

'But she probably had the opportunity, with Mr Pritchard away. And she could have called on you if she needed help.' For a moment, the possibility of the devoted younger brother, helping a sister driven to desperate action, seemed to Rushton the likeliest scenario for this death.

Brooke shook his head stubbornly. 'She didn't do it. I'd have had more reason to do it than her.'

Rushton ignored that for the moment. 'What about her husband? Mark Warner doesn't seem to have had much more time for your mother than you did.'

'Mark didn't like her.' His eyes brightened momentarily at the thought. 'I doubt whether he killed her, though. He's got more sense than that.' It was an unexpected return to an adult bearing.

'Did you kill her, Peter?'

Rushton thought that the sudden switch would throw his man once again off balance, that the suggestion might even outrage him. But he was disappointed. Brooke flashed him a quick look from the dark eyes. 'No. I don't think I could murder anyone. Least of all my own mother—perhaps I shouldn't have said I hated her.'

'No. Where were you in the week when she was killed?' He was hamstrung like the rest of the investigating officers by the absence of a precise time of death.

'In London. All that week.'

'Is there anyone who can witness that for you?'

Peter Brooke smiled. A sense of irony was a luxury he had almost forgotten—he found himself enjoying its return. 'Not unless you count a few thousand London Transport customers. I was busking on the Underground, I expect.'

Rushton was rattled. How could you expect to pin anyone down, when there was a full week to account for? He said, 'What about the nights? There must be someone who can at least vouch for your presence in London then.'

Brooke was immediately on the defensive. 'No. Not really. We live our own lives, you see. We don't notice what other people are up to.' If he brought pigs sniffing round the squat, he might lose his place there. None of them wanted that, and some of the people there would certainly have more to hide than he had. 'I've told you all I can. I don't know the people who've been around my mother during these last years.' The appeal in his voice turned it into almost a whine.

Rushton said firmly, 'We shall need an address for you. When we have a more definite time of death, we shall be questioning you more closely about your movements at that time. It will be in your own interest to produce someone who can vouch for those movements, if you can.'

Brooke looked past him, staring from his hunched posture at the blank wall three feet behind his interrogator. 'I hope you get the man who killed her. You were right: murder is a foul thing. No one deserves to be garrotted to death like that.' He sounded suddenly completely desolate; he was preparing to become Jake again.

Rushton was almost back in Gloucestershire when he fell to wondering who had told Peter Brooke just how his mother had been killed.


CHAPTER TWELVE

The funeral director found James Pritchard an ideal customer. Where so many of the distressed bereaved were vague, he was commendably precise. Where they dithered, he was calm and decisive, entirely clear-sighted about the arrangements for his wife's last journey.

Laura, he explained, had outlined to him the arrangements she would like, even though she had not expected to die for many years yet. She wanted none of the maudlin business with a clergyman intoning solemnly at a graveside; no relatives casting earth upon a coffin lowered into its pit. A cremation, it would be, with a few brisk words from the vicar of the church the Pritchards had visited twice a year. There would be just three verses of 'Abide with Me', Laura Pritchard's favourite hymn—her husband was so confident about this that the undertaker saw no reason on this occasion to point out that some of the older mourners might see an inappropriate association with the FA Cup Final. Then the small party would move briskly away to a short reception at the Feathers: there would be no need for anything elaborate, since no one would be travelling very far.

Moreover, there would be ample profit, without the tiresome exertions sometimes compelled upon funeral directors by the indecisions of less reliable mourners. There would be only one official car behind the hearse, but that was quite usual in these days of universal motoring. And Mr Pritchard had chosen the most expensive casket and fittings, without even pausing to compare prices. There would not be many visitors to the Chapel of Rest at the funeral parlour: when the body was eventually released by the police, it was not to be available for viewing. The funeral director was privately much relieved; it was what he would have advised, had his advice been sought. It would have challenged even his skilled embalmers to have made that shattered corpse fit for a dignified inspection by those who came to grieve. Much better to screw down the casket lid and leave any visitors who came to meditate among the lilies and the soft electronic music.

The undertaker recorded these arrangements in the hardbacked black book he brought with him on these occasions. Write everything down immediately: that was the first precept he impressed upon his staff. People who were upset often forgot what they had ordered, especially when the time came to present the bills. It was as well to have your own complete record of everything they had agreed with the benefit of expert advice.

He did not think there would be problems of that kind here—James Pritchard was so very definite. Shutting his book and returning his fountain pen to the inside pocket of his dark suit, the funeral director did not venture to wonder how deep was the grief of this man for his wife. That would have been quite unprofessional.

The presence of the funeral director meant that Lambert and Hook had to wait for a few minutes to see Jim Pritchard. They could hear Pritchard's clipped, almost military tones and the undertaker's deferential, reverent replies, without distinguishing a word of either through the thick oak door of the sitting-room.

Lambert, not caring to be thought an eavesdropper, eventually strode out on to the drive and began to inspect the outside of the house. They had made an appointment to see Pritchard at this time; it was irritating to find him otherwise engaged when they arrived, even if funeral arrangements were a regrettable necessity. The unworthy thought that Pritchard might be deliberately playing the situation for sympathy slipped into his mind. If he was, it wouldn't work.

On a day like this, The Beeches emphasized the qualities for which British gardens are famous. The sun blazed from a cloudless sky; the huge 'Pink Pearl' rhododendron near the gate was a twenty-foot high mound of exotic flowers; the lawns curved away in emerald swathes among the weedless beds. Everton Smith might have aroused the ire of the formidable lady of this house on one occasion, but no one could fault his diligence or his work rate, if one was to judge by the present state of the gardens. Unless, of course, this was the work of the dead woman herself, who was known to be an enthusiast for her garden.

As if he picked up the thought, Hook said, 'Laura Pritchard couldn't have given this lawn its latest mowing, nor cut that hedge. She's been dead for a fortnight now.'

They were silent for a moment, considering how nature, even organized, disciplined nature like this, emphasized the transience of man and his efforts. Blackbirds and thrushes sang their delight in the pleasant warmth, the water lilies were out on the pond beside them, the tops of the firs at the end of the garden were absolutely motionless in the gathering heat. This seemed more than ever a strange place for violent death to originate.

Then death's representative emerged in his dark suit through the wide front doorway of the house, as if to emphasize that the lady who had once ruled this dominion so forcefully would appear here no more. The funeral director regarded them for a moment with the mournful curiosity of a Dickensian mute, then climbed into his car and crunched away cautiously over the gravel. He used a speed in keeping with his calling while he remained within the boundaries of this house of bereavement; then they heard him accelerate away on the more anonymous roads beyond the gate.

When the policemen turned back to the house, they found the man who had brought them here regarding them steadily from the open doorway. James Pritchard seemed perfectly at ease.

When they had given him the news of his wife's death at the airport, they had interviewed him in a small, windowless room, studying his reactions at close quarters, as if he were a specimen under a microscope. On his own ground, he seemed determined to prove that it was he who was in control of the situation. 'Do come inside, gentlemen,' he called. 'We can talk in my study.' Bert Hook felt as though he were about to be interviewed for a job.

Lambert always expected studies to be lined with books. He found that increasingly they were not. This one had the seemingly obligatory computer and printer dominating the leather-topped desk. There was an angled metal study lamp between the printer and the monitor screen. The books were confined to a single two-foot shelf on the wall beside the desk; there was a concise Oxford dictionary, a thesaurus, three more reference volumes and a cluster of technical journals. The room, with its polished panelling extending to half the height of the high walls, had been designed for an earlier age, when carriages trundled over the gravel outside its window to the stable which was now a garage.

There were expensive hi-fi speakers on either side of the window, with the radio and CD player stacked in the hearth where no fire had burned in many years. Lambert wondered if this was one of those rooms where a man played at being busy, rather than did much actual work. But the chairs they were invited to sit in were comfortable enough, and the room, being on the north side of the house, was cool, despite the sun outside.

Pritchard waited until they had taken the armchairs he offered before pulling out his desk chair to face them. As he sat down, he said, 'May I ask if you have made much progress in finding my wife's murderer?'

It was as unemotional as a man inquiring about the sale of a house. Lambert said, 'We've narrowed the field of the investigation.'

Pritchard's eyes tightened very slightly; his faint smile beneath the two inches of black moustache did not diminish. 'I take that to mean that you are not yet near an arrest. Does it also mean that you've discarded the idea that this was a random killing by someone who had no previous connection with Laura?'

Lambert, determinedly unruffled by this calm detachment in a bereaved spouse, smiled back. 'I thought *I* was supposed to ask the questions. But I'll be quite honest with you, Mr Pritchard. We have not yet eliminated the possibility of an unplanned murder on the lines you suggest. My own opinion is that our man or woman will come from the small circle of people who knew your wife well.'

'Really. Someone in her employ, or someone who had enjoyed her confidence for years, perhaps.'

'Or a relative.'

Pritchard's knuckles tightened on the arms of his leather swivel chair, then visibly relaxed again, as if accepting his brain's message that they must do so. 'That is possible, I suppose. I hope that you are wrong.' It was an oblique, perhaps unconscious, way of telling them that he did not regard himself as one of their possibilities among relatives.

Lambert thought it was time to disturb this irritating calm. 'You told us that your wife was an active member of the Cathedral Choir, Mr Pritchard. I think you thought that she was attending their meetings at least once and sometimes more than once in each week.'

'Yes. Have you investigated her contacts there?'

'We have indeed. Would it surprise you to know that she has not been to a choir meeting for well over a year?'

Pritchard certainly looked surprised. He said stupidly, 'Are—are you sure of that?' in a wholly convincing manner.

Lambert ignored the question. 'Now that you know that, have you any idea where she could have been on those occasions?' He knew himself that she had been with the brisk and capable Sue Hendry, but he wanted to know if Jim Pritchard also suspected that that was where his wife had been.

A darkening of what might have been anger passed across the man's round, bronzed face; it was so fleeting that it was impossible to be certain what emotion had prompted it. His voice was suddenly harsh as he said, 'Are you suggesting that Laura was seeing another man?'

'I'm asking if you can think of any reason why she should have chosen to deceive you in this way.'

'You mean another man, though. That's the most usual reason for women lying to their husbands, isn't it? You lot must see plenty of that!' He gave them a smile which was at once bitter and aggressive, as if they were in some way responsible for the frailties of humanity which they turned up during an investigation. It was a reaction they met often enough.

'It's a common reason, certainly—the most common one, as you suggest. But there are others.' Lambert wondered whether to suggest to this conventional man in his comfortable bourgeois house that the source of his wife's secret passion might be a woman. 'Forgive me for asking my next question, but I hope you will see that it is inevitable. Has your own marriage been a happy one in the last year or so?'

'Happy enough, yes. I told you that when you met me at the airport.' Pritchard's features set into a sullen mask and he looked at the carpet, not at his questioner.

'That is not a very informative phrase. Was the marriage happy enough for you to feel now that your wife was not looking for some kind of relationship outside it?'

For a moment as Pritchard looked up, they saw the man he had sought to hide from them. His lips flared suddenly like a dog's when it snarls, his teeth flashed white against the blackness of the moustache above them. 'You mean was it good in bed, don't you? Why not come straight out with it? Well, it was all right. I told you that before. Sex wasn't as good or as frequent as it had been at first, but that's marriage, isn't it? Neither of us was a teenager; I suppose we expected it to cool a bit as the years went on.'

Lambert reflected that he was talking like a long-married man, when this marriage had lasted scarcely four years. He wanted to learn everything he could about this man's sex life, not from any prurient interest, but because it might have a bearing on the way his wife's death had come about. But he could not probe it in any more detail, not at this stage. He said, 'I'm sure you want us to arrest your wife's murderer as quickly as possible. You must see that it is vital that we know who, if anyone, she was meeting on those occasions when she chose to deceive you about her whereabouts.'

Pritchard paused, giving every appearance of according

a painful matter his full consideration. Then he said, 'No, I'm sorry. If she was meeting someone, I don't know who it was.'

In the quiet, high room Pritchard's uneven breathing was the only discernible sound. It was Hook who looked up from his notebook to say, 'What do you know about the people who worked for your wife?'

Again there was a sharp flicker of emotion across Pritchard's bronzed face. It did not look like fear. It might have been shock, but this was surely a question the man should have expected. Perhaps he was surprised by the sudden switch of questioner rather than by this new subject—he had almost forgotten Hook's presence. He said slowly, 'I know very little. I have only been to her office once, or perhaps twice. Secretarial services are something I hire, as I need them in my own business, but otherwise know very little about. Laura knew what she needed in her staff at Worcester—I didn't see it as my function to intervene.'

Lambert looked hard for a double meaning in these last sentiments. He sought to catch a trace of irony in the words, but he could detect none. He said, 'But you would know Mrs Pritchard's manager, Sue Hendry?'

'I wouldn't say know her. I think I was introduced to her when I visited the place.' For the first time, there was just a hint of disgust; it came in the way he delivered that phrase 'the place'. Lambert reflected that Jim Pritchard must almost certainly recollect the brisk Miss Hendry more vividly than he pretended to. With her red hair and green eyes, her sturdy figure and her slightly aggressive air, she was no neutral, quickly forgotten figure.

'But your wife seems to have had a close working and social relationship with Miss Hendry.' It was as far as he was prepared to push it at the moment, though he despised his carefully chosen words even as he delivered them.

'I suppose you would expect that in a small firm. But we didn't discuss our work much at home. There was an unspoken agreement between us that we didn't bring our problems into the house.' Perhaps the man knew no more than he was showing; perhaps on the other hand he knew very much more. Everything he said seemed to be designed to keep them at arm's length, to protect his own feelings from their intrusions. He was like an expert fencer, watching the ground beneath his feet, measuring his defence, assessing his opponent's strengths and weaknesses.

And it was indeed possible he knew nothing of the relationship or the woman involved. Sue Hendry had certainly not suggested that she knew much of the third side of the unusual eternal triangle in which she had become involved. Lambert said, 'We need your help. You must know your wife's movements, the places she visited often, better than we do. Have you any idea where she might have been killed?'

Pritchard looked a little surprised, perhaps a little relieved, as if he thought this was safer ground. 'No. I've thought about that, but I can't suggest anywhere. Is it important?'

'Oh, yes. When an attack on someone takes place, there is almost invariably what police jargon calls "an exchange" between the attacker and the victim and the surrounding terrain. Something significant will be left behind for our forensic people. It can be hair, skin, clothing, blood, or even just indents in the earth.' Usually, he would have withheld such detail from a bereaved spouse. This time there seemed no need to protect this man who seemed so little affected by his wife's death from the facts of a murder investigation.

'Yes, I see that. But there isn't anywhere I can suggest as a possible place for murder. You obviously didn't find anything significant near Laura's body?'

'There was nothing near the part of the river where she was found, no. But the corpse had been in the water for some days, and had almost certainly drifted down the river in that time. In any case, we know that your wife was dead long before she went into the water. She was taken there after she had been killed. That is why, as you will be aware, we have been examining the vehicles of anyone who we know was connected with your late wife. Including your own Jaguar and your wife's car.'

Pritchard was thoroughly composed again now. Lambert was searching for any signs of distress or alarm in the dark brown eyes as he delivered these facts, but he saw none. Pritchard said with a sardonic smile, 'I could hardly not be aware. My Jaguar was the first car you cleared.' That showed his confidence: no one as yet had informed him officially that the Jaguar was in fact clean, but in fact nothing incriminating had been found within it.

Lambert said abruptly, 'What can you tell us about your wife's first husband, Mr Pritchard?'

It was another sudden switch, and this time his man did look disconcerted. 'Very little. Laura's marriage was effectively at an end before I arrived on the scene.' It was a familiar disclaimer, which might or might not be true; even at the end of this turbulent century, few people liked to admit to being agents in the disruption of a marriage. Second spouses always preferred to see themselves as picking up the pieces rather than smashing the fragile human porcelain. 'Brooke died a year after Laura left him. We didn't marry until two years after that.' He folded his arms with the air of a man who had disposed of a topic of conversation.

'Yet your late wife's son seems to have resented her conduct.'

Pritchard shrugged. 'Peter is an odd chap, by all accounts. I hardly know him: I refused to get involved in any arguments between him and Laura. As a stepfather, you can't win.'

That at any rate was almost certainly true. Lambert decided to reveal a little of their findings, in the hope of a reaction. 'Peter Brooke was still very bitter against his mother at the time of her death. He has admitted as much to one of my officers.'

'He was very attached to his father, I believe: always closer to him than to his mother, according to Laura. David Brooke died of cancer six years ago. I think Peter still held Laura responsible for that death, just as he blamed her for everything that went wrong for his father. Over the last year or two, he's been living as a real drop-out in London. We didn't even know his address for most of the time—not that that bothered me.'

Pritchard, who must have known that Peter Brooke was an obvious murder suspect, had made no real attempt to suggest his guilt, though Lambert had offered him the possibility as something of a trap. He said, 'When was the last time that Peter Brooke was with his mother? Do you know?'

Pritchard pursed his lips; his air that of a man trying to be as helpful as he could. 'I think he came to see her in the week before I went on my golfing holiday. I don't know what about.'

If that was correct, it could be very significant. Both Brooke and his sister had told them that his last meeting with his mother had been weeks earlier. Lambert, as studiously unconcerned as Pritchard appeared to be, said, 'Could you recall exactly which day that was, for Sergeant Hook's record?'

Pritchard furrowed the brow which seemed loftier beneath his receding hair. The sun had burnt the tender area around his hairline on his Spanish holiday, and the skin was peeling a little; he raised a hand and rubbed it, as though this was an aid to thought. 'No, I'm sorry, but I couldn't be precise about the day. Thursday or Friday before I left on the Saturday, I think. Perhaps Lau—perhaps his sister, Joyce, could tell you. I wasn't around when he came here.' He looked suddenly more animated. 'That puts it only a few days before the murder, doesn't it? I can see why you would find it interesting, but I'm afraid I can't pinpoint the actual time for you.'

Lambert was interested in the way he placed the murder firmly in the days after he had departed for Spain. But of course, that is exactly what an innocent man would do. The superintendent wished once again that they could establish an exact time for this killing. He would like at least to eliminate this calm figure before them from the inquiry. That came not from any predilection in Pritchard's favour, but merely because he was too well-organized to have as an opponent.

At a nod from his chief, Hook produced a scrap of stationery from his briefcase. He passed it across the small space between them and said, 'Is that your wife's handwriting, Mr Pritchard?'

Jim Pritchard read the note aloud, as if that would help him to digest it. *I'll be away this week, after all. Sorry I couldn't let you know earlier. See you next Tuesday as usual. Laura Pritchard.* He looked at it for several seconds after he had read out the few simple words, as if they carried a hidden meaning which he might discover. Then he said dully, 'Yes. That's Laura's writing. And that's her signature. Was it left for the cleaner? She usually comes on Tuesdays.'

'Yes. Mrs Evans gave our officers that note. It was waiting for her here on the Tuesday after you left for Spain. Of course, she came as the note suggests she should on the following Tuesday, but there was no one here. Your wife had been dead for several days at least by then.'

'Yes, I see that. But presumably she was alive until the Tuesday morning, when she left this note.' For the first time, he seemed near to tears. He kept his eyes on the scrap of paper which he held still in his hand; perhaps the pathos of the few innocent phrases in his wife's hand was bringing her death home to him at last.

'It would appear so, yes. Is this the first time you have seen this note?'

He looked puzzled. 'Yes. I was away when it was written.'

'Quite. And have you any idea where she planned to spend these days away from home?'

'No. When I went off abroad, I was sure she was planning

to spend the time at The Beeches. Do you think this trip is connected with her disappearance?'

'Obviously it might be. Can you make any suggestion as to whom she might have been planning to meet?'

'No.' He looked down again at the note, as if he could crack its code and produce the vital information. 'It doesn't say here that she was planning to meet anyone, of course.'

'But nor had she indicated to you that she was planning to go off alone. We have to face the possibility that any person she met might have killed her, or might know who killed her.'

If Pritchard knew that his wife had been planning to meet her female lover, he still gave no sign. He seemed to be fighting for control of himself, but his tone remained even as he said, 'No doubt if that is so you will find that person in due course.'

Lambert said, 'Mr Pritchard, what can you tell us about your gardener, Everton Smith?'

Perhaps Jim Pritchard was still preoccupied with conjecture about what his wife had planned in his absence; he was silent for so long that it began to seem that he had not heard the question. Then he said in a low voice, 'Very little. I saw him when he had temporary work at the golf club— you could scarcely call it an interview. I knew from the green-keeper that his work there had been satisfactory. I offered him a full day's work each week here and he jumped at it. After that, Laura saw far more of him than me: she's— she was the gardener, you see.' He looked through the open window at the evidence of that interest, as though noticing it for the first time.

They followed his gaze and, as if in response to their attention, the phone in Lambert's car shrilled through the bird song, and Hook went out to answer its insistent tones. They listened to his large feet hastening noisily over the gravel before Lambert said, 'Did Mrs Pritchard find his work here as satisfactory as that you had seen at the golf club?' He had picked up Pritchard's adjective, repeating it as if it had some special significance.

'I think so, yes. They had that one disagreement, which I told you about, when Smith removed some of her plants because he thought they were weeds. It was a mistake anyone without specialist knowledge might have made, but Laura had quite a temper, I'm afraid.'

'But you don't think that row has any significance for us now?'

'No, I'm sure it hasn't. I can assure you that the lad wouldn't still be working here if Laura had thought it a serious breach. But you can ask him yourself, Superintendent. That is the noise of his chariot now, unless I'm much mistaken.'

They heard the roar of the Honda 750 many seconds before it appeared; their ears followed a series of expert gear changes until the white motorcycle rolled slowly to a halt over the gravel, still invisible on the other side of the house. The noise allowed Bert Hook to return to the room almost in silence, so that his large presence filled the doorway before they were aware of it.

'That was DI Rushton,' he said. 'He's had a report from forensic which he thought we might like to know about while we were here.' He looked from Pritchard to his chief, waiting until the tiny nod from Lambert told him that he could reveal this information. Then he said, 'It seems that Mrs Pritchard's body was taken to the river in the boot of her own car.'

## CHAPTER THIRTEEN

Joyce Warner was usually pleased to see her husband when he popped in unexpectedly for lunch. Today she was hoping desperately that he would not come back to the house. She did not like having secrets from her husband, but it was better for both of them that he did not know about this.

She found herself looking repeatedly at the clock as the morning went on; her nervousness was reflected in the sharp way she checked the children when they became fractious with each other. She put Tim in his cot for a sleep at ten-thirty, and was pleased to find when she crept in ten minutes later that he had dropped off; his face was round and innocent, unlined as a doll's. She would have to take him with her, so it was better that he rested now.

At eleven-thirty, Mark rang from the office to tell her that a long overdue payment had come in. It felt like a bonus to both of them: they had been sure the firm concerned was going into receivership, that Warner Plastics would never be paid. It was only two thousand, but it seemed another omen of better things to come, a confirmation of the new era ushered in by her mother's death.

'I just thought you'd like to know,' said Mark, underlining again how close they were, how open with each other about the things which happened to them. She felt a traitor even as they spoke. But before she rang off, she managed to elicit the information that he was lunching with a customer.

She made sure the children ate, but she could manage only a mug of tea and a biscuit herself. At one-fifteen, she dropped Katie at the nursery school, watching with a mother's mixture of joy and regret as the child ran happily into the single-storey building without a backward glance.

She checked again that Tim was safe in his car seat and then set off for Gloucester. Listening to his cheerful burblings behind her as she drove, she felt a pang of remorse that she should involve such innocence in a secretive rendezvous like this. But she had no choice—there was nowhere she could have left him without concocting some unconvincing story about her purposes. And another, unworthy part of her mind—the part she was trying to suppress—told her that a toddler was the best possible cover for this meeting. Strangers seeing them in the streets might even take the man she was to meet for Tim's father—she smiled wryly at that thought.

There were other, smaller places where they could have met. She had chosen Gloucester for the anonymity of a city. It was not a city like London, of course, or even Oxford, but it was a bustling, busy place, where people did not have much time to study those who passed them in the streets.

She did not like multi-storey car parks, but Tim cheered happily behind her as they swung round the tight left-hand turns and spiralled upwards to the fourth floor and a parking space. She looked at her watch as they descended to street level in the lift. They had better not be late.

The man they were meeting was too nervous to be left for long.

In the large garden shed at The Beeches, Everton Smith was making a great play of removing the plug from the large cylinder mower. It saved him from looking into the faces of the detectives.

The snag with this tactic was that the CID men knew exactly what he was about, registered the evasion, and immediately began to conjecture about the reason for it. They watched the top of his dark head as he bent to the task, knowing that eventually he must look up into their faces if they chose not to offer him further questions. The tensions were all on his side, and eventually he must succumb to them.

They had followed Smith out here because Pritchard had hovered protectively about his employee in the house, as if anxious to watch how he behaved under their questioning. It was no doubt a natural curiosity in a bereaved husband, but if necessary Lambert would have asked Pritchard to remove himself, even in his own house. The contradictions in suspects' accounts were often the most significant items—and James Pritchard remained a suspect, even if it seemed that his absence at the time of death might make him no more than an accessory.

But Pritchard was not a stupid man; he took the hint when they said they were going to see Smith in the garden and left them to it. The young black man seemed curiously reluctant to leave the house, although from both their accounts he and the owner had scarcely seen each other since Pritchard had offered him the gardening job, so that they could hardly know each other well. But Smith was nervous and suspicious of the police, as they had seen even on his home ground; probably he considered that the presence of his eminently middle-class employer offered some sort of protection against whatever ordeal was in store for him.

In an attempt to put Smith at his ease, Lambert indicated to his detective sergeant that he should begin the questioning. Bert Hook said, 'Bike must be useful for getting to a place like this, Everton. You've always come here on the Honda, I expect?'

It was not as artless and introductory as it seemed. Judging by the noise of Smith's arrival today, it was probable that any unscheduled visits would have been noticed by someone in the village. Smith merely nodded his answer, as if he did not trust himself to speak. But perhaps it was them he did not trust; young blacks who have grown up in Birmingham do not accept the police at face value. He said reluctantly, as if he suspected a trap he could not divine, 'Yes. Makes travelling a pleasure, she does. Well, you couldn't get here without your own transport, could you?'

'Indeed you couldn't, unless you lived round here and could walk.' It was a fact which was relevant to this death, now that it seemed that the victim might well have died here before she was taken to the river in her own car.

'You can obviously handle that bike, Everton. I presume you can drive a car as well,' said Hook.

'Yeah, course I can. Was going to get me a job, being able to drive, wasn't it?' He smiled at the bitter irony of the thought, pleased with it in spite of himself. Irony was an effect not often attempted in Everton Smith's world. Then he looked at Hook suspiciously, fearing that vanity might have led him into an indiscretion.

'But you always came here on the Honda?'

'Yes. I'm not stupid enough to pinch cars.'

'And far too honest, no doubt.' Hook, exuding stolidity like a protective disguise, also enjoyed the occasional irony. 'How often do you come to The Beeches, Everton?'

'Once a week in winter, twice a week from Easter to the end of October.' The formula came so pat that he had obviously used it before: probably it had been for him the most important phrase in the original verbal agreement.

'So twice a week at present. Which days?'

'Usually a Tuesday afternoon and a Friday morning. But it varies a bit—I've come other times as well.'

'Yes. You told us when we saw you before. When the black economy offers you other unofficial work, you're permitted to vary your times to allow you to go elsewhere.'

Smith looked sullen. 'Within reason, so long as I give reasonable notice of any change.' The pitch of his voice showed that he was carefully recalling the dead woman's wording. Her precise phrases came suddenly clearly to them from this strange source, as if they had caught a fleeting glimpse of her through distant trees. 'But it wasn't just me: sometimes I came at other times to fit in with Mrs Pritchard's arrangements. She liked to be here when I was, to work with me, see?'

'I see. Ever since the day when you pulled out some of her plants by mistake, was it?'

His face fell, as clearly as that of a child reminded of some ancient misdemeanour he hoped had been forgotten. 'That was about the only time I worked without her,' he confessed.

'Which means that you saw Laura Pritchard once a week throughout the winter and twice a week for the last eight weeks or so. More often than all except a very few people—

probably more often than her family, apart from Mr Pritchard.'

Smith looked surprised. 'I suppose so.'

'And did your relationship ever go beyond that of employer and employee?' Hook looked at the smooth, uncomprehending features. 'Did you become friends, Everton? Did you become lovers?' Trying not to see Lambert as he studied the incredulity on the other side of the big mower, he asked desperately, 'Were you giving her one, Everton? It's not unknown, and you know it.'

Smith looked at him for another moment. Then his face cracked into a grin which seemed all white teeth, a grin in which amusement at the idea swiftly overcame his initial outrage. 'You got some strange ideas, man.' He guyed the relaxed West Indian speech of his father, which he had often envied but never found natural in himself. 'Yo' read all these things about black men's ding-a-lings being bigger and better, about how respectable white women just caaan't resist us, man! And yo' think young Everton's dipping his bread with the fine lady. Well, let me tell you, it ain't true. But don't you stop spreadin' it around, just 'cause of that.' He dropped the cameo abruptly, as if he had suddenly remembered the calling of the men he was addressing.

Hook said stiffly, 'It's nothing to do with colour. It's not unknown for older women to fancy a roll with young limbs. Sometimes they take their pleasures wherever they can find them; just like a lot of men, in fact.'

Smith nodded, still amused. But he did not resume his parody of Caribbean tones as he said, 'Fancy a bit of rough, you mean. Yeah, I'm sure it happens. But it didn't here. If you'd known the lady, you wouldn't even have asked.'

'But we didn't know her, you see, Everton. That's why we had to ask. We're dependent on people like you for the picture we get of her. Fierce lady, was she, Mrs Pritchard?'

Smith thought for a moment. The sparking plug was back in the mower now, and he wiped his oily hands on a piece of rag. This unhurried physical movement seemed to calm the febrile excitement which had been increasingly evident in his previous reactions. 'No, not really, when you got to know her. She seemed a very severe woman at first, but when she got to know you she was quite different. She was fair. Once you realized you weren't going to get away with skimping things—that's what she called it when we talked—she left you quite a lot to yourself. I think in the end she trusted me to work without much supervision from her.'

Despite himself, despite the fact that he would have denied it fiercely to his friends, he was proud of the fact that a middle-aged woman had trusted him, had believed that he would not slack even if the chance came. Everton Smith put a high value on trust, because he had not enjoyed very much of it in his short adult life.

'Who do you think killed her, Everton?'

Hook threw it in almost casually when Smith had displayed some feeling for his employer, and the young face with its delicately handsome features was immediately blanked with caution. 'Don't know, do I? How could I know?'

Hook paused, noted the caution, flung out his next question as though it was a brutal weapon. 'Did you steal from her, Everton? Take money from the house, when she wasn't around?'

'No! Ain't ever taken things like that, not from anyone.' His indignation crashed like stones off the wooden walls of the shed. His outrage did not include surprise: men like him expected to be accused of theft, whenever anything around them was missing. 'Anyway, I told you. I wasn't left here on my own. Hardly ever.'

Hook carried on as if he had not even heard the protestation. 'Did Mrs Pritchard find you'd taken things, Everton? Did you kill her to shut her up, when she accused you?'

'No! No, you're on the wrong track. I never laid a finger on her.' The fear showed in Smith's wide eyes. 'You can't fit me up with this!' He did not sound either convinced or convincing.

Bert Hook wished the whole of the CID section could see him weighing into this startled young man. That would have killed the jibes about him favouring the underdog. Yet Lambert, watching this forcefulness, thought how mild Hook's attitude was compared with that of some of the men on his section. It was the superintendent who now said quietly, 'Then where did the money come from, Mr Smith?'

As he turned to face this new threat, Smith's pupils shone black in the dim light of the hut. But the whites of them were getting ever wider—he looked like a trapped animal. Now Lambert's quiet voice tolled its facts like a knell in his ear. 'You paid off the remaining instalments on your motorbike a fortnight ago. Well over a thousand pounds. Just before Mrs Pritchard died. Don't bother to make things worse by denying it: finance companies have to open their records to the police, when we're investigating serious crime.'

Lambert's matter-of-fact tone unnerved Smith as much as the facts he was presented with. 'I—I work hard. I don't spend much, you know. I had—had a bit of luck on the horses.'

'Oh, Everton, you can do better than that, surely. That's too old a tale for even a young lad like you to think we might believe it.'

'I didn't steal the money,' he said sullenly, with his eyes cast down.

'Then how did you come by it?'

Smith opened his mouth, but no words came, even in the silence which they stretched like an accusation. He shook his head stubbornly.

'We're going to need an answer, you know; you must see that.' Lambert watched the young features setting like marble, then moved out into the sunlight. Smith followed his two tormentors as if attached to them by a string. Lambert looked up at the house; there was no sign of Jim

Pritchard. 'When did you last see Mrs Pritchard alive, Mr Smith?'

The gardener appreciated the implication of the adjective, but he had no idea how to react to it. Eventually he said hoarsely, 'Monday afternoon. The one after Mr Pritchard went off on holiday. She said to come then rather than Tuesday, because she might be going away.'

Lambert and Hook donned their professional inscrutability, automatically concealing the fact that this was vital information. For the first time, they were going to be able to place the time of death with some accuracy, especially as no one in the village had come up with a later sighting than this. There had been considerable deterioration of the corpse in the river, which meant that Laura Pritchard could not have lived much beyond that Monday afternoon when she had worked here with Smith. Probably she had died in the twenty-four or thirty-six hours after that.

'Did she seem normal to you on that afternoon?'

'Normal?' Smith was suddenly obtuse.

'Yes. Did she seem preoccupied? Apprehensive? Nervous about anything? On edge in any way?' Irritation mounted in Lambert's tones with the repetitive phrases.

'No. She was normal.' The slim shoulders turned away from them, and Lambert almost reached out to swing him back face to face, wishing in that moment that he had the man in an interview room.

But Hook was watching their quarry: he had moved round to the other side of him, his steps noisy on the gravel, so that when Smith began to walk he looked almost as though he was under arrest. They caught a glimpse now of Jim Pritchard's high-domed face, staring curiously at this ill-assorted threesome from the drawing-room of his house. Lambert said, 'Think carefully about this next question, Mr Smith: it will be very much in your own interest to give us whatever information you can. Do you know of any person or persons who was an enemy of Mrs Pritchard?'

'No.' The monosyllable came on the heels of the last

word of the question, despite the injunction that he should take his time. As if he realized his mistake, Smith said clumsily, 'She seemed all right to me. I didn't know her all that well, you know.'

'What did you do that afternoon?'

'I mowed the lawns and cut the edges. Takes a good two hours, that.' Again the answer tumbled out too readily, as if he had been waiting for the question. They were walking on those lawns now, almost as far away from the house as they could get.

'And what did Mrs Pritchard do?'

This time Smith did not speak immediately; his stride faltered for a moment, as if reflecting the confusion in his mind. 'I—I'm not sure. She was in the house for part of the time.'

'But you said she usually worked with you, Everton.' This was Hook, gently insistent, his voice a little puzzled, as if he was concerned to keep his notebook records of these things clear.

'I think she did a bit of weeding. And—and she was in the greenhouse. Yes, that's it—I remember now. She was in the greenhouse, getting the bedding plants ready to plant out.'

That innocent structure was beside them as he spoke, for they had turned back now from the laurels at the boundary of the garden. All three of them turned and looked at its glass walls, as if they could confirm the words of the speaker. Lambert said, 'And exactly where did you last see Mrs Pritchard alive, Mr Smith?'

'On the steps at the back of the house.'

'And she paid you your money?'

For an instant, there was panic on his face. Then it cleared, as if he had suddenly understood their meaning, and he said, 'Yes. She paid me in cash. She always did that.' He stared hard at the ground. At that moment, he seemed near to tears. The emotion did nothing to clear him in their eyes. Weeping reflected guilt or remorse or even extreme tension quite as often as mere compassion, in the extraordinary experience of the CID.

They were standing now by the steps on which he claimed he had had this last exchange with the dead woman. Hook said with gentle insistence, 'And you didn't notice anything unusual in her manner or what she said as you left her here?'

'No. She was normal.' He stared hard at the bottom of the three steps. Again the negative had come too quickly upon the heels of the question to carry conviction; he was refusing even to contemplate the suggestion they were putting to him. To Lambert, he sounded in his stubbornness like Peter denying his Christ; that fanciful thought set the superintendent wondering again how close this relationship between a middle-aged, middle-class woman and her young working-class employee had been.

'And presumably she said that she would see you as usual when you came back later in the week?'

Smith glanced up at the simple question with something very like panic in his eyes. Perhaps he was convinced now that they were trying to trap him. Or perhaps he really had something to hide. 'No. I think she was going away, from what she said. But I told her I didn't want to come twice in that week.'

'Why?'

They had expected him to hesitate, but the answer came pat. 'I had some other work on.'

'What other work?'

'I was decorating. Painting a house. I can take you there, if you want me to. Bloke wanted it done before the weekend, so I couldn't take the time off to come to The Beeches. I told Mrs Pritchard, and she said it would be all right, so long as I didn't miss more than one of my days.' From saying too little too quickly, he had moved to offering almost too much; the phrases tumbled out, as if he was glad to have the explanation to hand. Perhaps he eventually realized how breathless he sounded, for his words stopped abruptly. He still carried the rag on which he had wiped the oil from his hands after cleaning the starting plug; he drew it incessantly through the fingers of one hand with the other, like a conjuror setting up a trick.

Lambert, conscious that Pritchard was again watching them from the window, said, 'We shall need to talk to you again in due course. You're going to tell us where that money came from, for one thing. However, we shall let you get on with your work now.' Smith's relief was manifest as he turned away from them. He had moved only a pace when Lambert said, 'Before you go, we need one more answer immediately. Did you see anyone around this house in the weeks before Mrs Pritchard's death whom you hadn't seen before?'

Smith turned back to them, his eyes narrowing a little against the sunlight on his right. 'I did see one man. Funny-looking bloke. He gave me quite a start when I turned the mower off. I hadn't noticed him until then. He was standing on the other side of my bike, you see, looking at it. For a moment, I thought he was thinking about pinching it.'

'And was he?'

'No. I don't think he was interested in it. He asked me if Mrs Pritchard was in. Said her name in a funny, deliberate sort of way, as if he thought it was funny.'

'Stressed it, you mean?'

'That's right. As if it had some meaning I didn't know about. Strange bloke, he was.'

'When was this?'

'That Monday, I think. When Mrs Pritchard was in the house. I asked him what he wanted, but he just shook his head. I put the mower away in the shed, and he wasn't there when I came out again.'

'What did he look like?'

'Tallish bloke. Long overcoat on, even though it was quite warm. Long hair. Scruffy shoes and trousers; and he was none too clean, I'd say, as if he'd been on the road, or sleeping rough.' Smith brought out the details with some eagerness, as though genuinely anxious now to be helpful. Perhaps he was relieved to be moving away from the areas of questioning which had distressed him.

'Old?'

'No, quite young. Not more than thirty. Perhaps less; they look older when they're scruffy, don't they? He was carrying something, in a sort of black box. Not very big, and it didn't seem heavy.'

Perhaps Everton Smith, bred on gangster films by a father who thought them ideal fare for young boys, suspected the mysterious visitor might have been carrying an automatic weapon. Lambert recalled Rushton's account of the interview he had conducted in London. He said slowly, 'Do you think it could have been a violin case?'

Smith's eyes widened for a moment in his face, then contracted to normal, as if he did not wish to acknowledge this surprising acuity in the police. But he could not keep a tiny touch of wonderment out of his voice as he said, 'Yeah. A violin case: that's what it was.'

The man was uneasy on the journey. There were not many passengers on the train; he had no one beside him or opposite him as he sat at the table and looked through the big window at the racing countryside. He had almost forgotten how green English fields could be during his years in the centre of the city. The Cotswolds were very lush at this time of the year; the cows stood motionless beneath the new canopies of leaf beside a lazy stream as if posing for a Constable. Everything seemed a prologue to the long summer days which lay ahead.

But he scarcely saw the scenes he would once have enjoyed. The high-speed train was rushing him far too rapidly towards the district his instincts told him he should avoid. And he was not used to having to keep still like this. He wanted to stand, to move about; but he had been to the toilet already, and he thought the few passengers had stared at him curiously as he moved down the centre aisle of the swaying carriage. He did not wish to attract their attention again.

When the train ran into Gloucester, he let the others who were alighting get out before him. As he shambled down the platform past the long chain of carriages, he undid the buttons on his long overcoat. It was much too hot for it this morning, but he did not think of taking it off; his father had always said that it was easier to carry a coat on your shoulders than over your arm. And he had other things to carry: a plastic carrier bag, as well as the instrument which went everywhere with him.

The man in the British Rail hat at the barrier seemed almost surprised to find that he had a ticket. He went out into the streets he had once known so well, half expecting to find people waiting there who knew him. But he met neither friendly greeting nor hostile challenge.

He had no need to ask the way. The streets were busier than he remembered them, and part of his route took him through a pedestrian precinct which had not existed when he last came here. But most of the tall buildings had been here since long before he was born, and he gathered a little confidence as he moved among them.

The cathedral was dark and cool after the sunlight in the close. He moved automatically towards the rich colours of the east window with its massive stone traceries, waiting for his eyes to adjust to the reduced light. Then he turned towards the spot where an enterprising Abbot had interred the body of Edward II in 1330, securing this ancient place as a centre of pilgrimage two centuries before it became a cathedral.

He had a moment of panic when he thought that she was not there. It was already after the time they had agreed. This was the place she had specified for their meeting, surely? Then he saw her, standing looking at the tomb with the child's hand in hers; there were no chairs here.

Joyce Warner slipped her other hand into her brother's as he moved beside her, then smiled encouragement into the anxious face above her. She said softly, 'We must get our story straight, Peter, if we are all to get the benefits of Mother's death.'

## CHAPTER FOURTEEN

The availability of capital was already apparent at Warner Plastics. It manifested itself in small things, but they were good for morale. Mark Warner's secretary had the new carpet and curtains in her office which she had despaired of ever achieving. She had even been offered a smart new notice for her door with the magic words 'Personal Assistant to Chief Executive', but she had said that her old title was good enough for her, unless there was a rise involved. And her employer was secretly pleased with her for her old-fashioned attitude, as she had known he would be.

Mark was putting the finishing touches to the company's smart new brochure on its products and services. He moved briefly among the men at their benches, letting them have their say on their specialisms, as was his wont. He was childishly pleased when they were impressed by the colour photography in the illustrations. He dared not tell them that a week ago it would have been impossible to contemplate even the modest expenditure involved in printing and distributing these brochures.

As soon as he returned to his office, his secretary announced Superintendent Lambert, and the sunlit day acquired a sudden chill. A moment later, the tall, dark-suited man filled his doorway, and Mark's overactive imagination was filled with images of messengers of doom. Lambert refused tea and sat down quietly in the armchair which was offered to him. Warner had the impression that his every move was being studied very closely; he could feel his sense of foreboding wrapping itself like a cloak around his shoulders. The CID man seemed in no hurry to speak; he waited still, watchful, expectant, until Mark settled himself at his desk.

Mark had determined that he would not begin the conversation, but eventually his nervousness made him say, 'And what can I do to help you, Mr Lambert?' He was conscious of forcing the smile which accompanied this opening banality.

Lambert said, 'You can tell me when you last visited The Beeches, for a start.'

'Oh, it must be some time ago, now. Six weeks or more, I suppose. I could try to check with Joyce, if it's important.' Mark was quite pleased with his insouciant delivery of this. Then he saw Lambert reaching into the side pocket of his jacket.

The object he produced was concealed for a moment in his large hand. Warner did not see it until Lambert leaned unhurriedly forward and placed it on the edge of his desk. 'Do you recognize this?' he said. His grey eyes had never left the other man's face throughout the manœuvre.

It was a ludicrously unthreatening object; why then did Mark feel his pulses quickening as he looked at it? He moved a hand to pick it up, then thought better of it, as if mere contact with the innocent thing could increase his danger. His hand lay awkwardly for a moment, palm upwards on his desk. Then he raised both his hands and ran them quickly through his yellow hair. 'There must be a thousand others around like that,' he said defensively.

Warner's eyes had fastened upon the object before him as if it held him by some sinister spell. Now Lambert's eyes dropped for the first time to look at the thing he had produced. It was a small model car. A BMW, a tiny version of the one Lambert had passed in its designated space on the way in. 'This one was found at The Beeches,' he said.

For a moment, Warner looked as if he would continue to deny the obvious. Then he said, 'It looks like one of Tim's—my son's—toys. He has a lot of cars. I expect he dropped it at his Granny's.' He produced the last word with an effort, as if even now the fact surprised him.

'Recently,' said Lambert calmly. It was a statement, not a question. His tone implied that a denial could only lead to further embarrassment.

'Why do you say that?'

Lambert had the air of a patient adult explaining a new concept to a child as he said, 'It was found in the open, in this condition. Had it been there for six weeks, it would certainly have needed a good clean to come up like this.'

Warner nodded, as if digesting a complex engineering idea. It was quite ridiculous, and Lambert was suddenly impatient with him. 'It was found by our Scene of Crime team, on the gravel path beside the garage at The Beeches. The garage housing Laura Pritchard's Astra. The car in which her body was transported to the Severn after she had been killed.'

The revelation had its effect. As Warner looked up into the face of his questioner, shock and fear flashed quickly into his too-revealing blue eyes. Perhaps the revelation about the macabre use of the dead woman's car had shaken him; perhaps he was merely disturbed that the police had discovered this use. Lambert followed up his advantage. 'There was a uniformed officer at The Beeches when you visited the house yesterday, Mr Warner. He watched you searching the grounds for a toy which was no longer there; it had been picked up with various other items of interest by our Scene of Crime team. What interests me is why you were so anxious to retrieve a toy car.'

Warner stared at the toy for a moment longer. Then he reached out his hand gingerly, put a finger on top of it, and rolled it slowly towards him, as if it were a snake whose venom had been suddenly removed. 'I was at the house more recently, as it seems you know.'

'When?'

'At around the time when my mother-in-law died. Perhaps on the very day. I didn't kill her.' There was an appeal in the last phrase, but it brought no response from Lambert.

'What day was that?'

'Sunday. The day after Jim Pritchard went away to Spain.'

Laura Pritchard had been alive until the following day at least, according to Everton Smith. 'Can anyone confirm that that was the day you went to the house?'

Warner looked surprised. He thought for a moment and said, 'No. I had Tim with me, but no one else. I didn't tell anyone else I was going, and I can't see a two-year-old being much use as a witness.'

'No. But without him and his toy car, we might never have known that you had been there at all. What was the purpose of this clandestine visit, Mr Warner?'

Warner sighed. 'I went to ask Laura for financial help with Warner Plastics. It's amazing how her death and the mere prospect of money has revived things, but I was quite desperate on that day. I took Tim because I thought the sight of a toddler and the knowledge that his future was at stake might make his grandmother provide the loan which we needed.'

'And was the move successful?'

'No. Knowing Laura, I doubt whether it would have been, even had I managed to put the proposition to her. But she was nowhere about. The place was locked and barred. She'd gone away.'

Lambert looked at him sharply. If Everton Smith was telling them the truth, Laura Pritchard had been at the house on the following day. 'Are you sure she wasn't just out of the house? What makes you think she'd gone away?'

Mark Warner thought for a moment, as if checking his facts and making sure there was no danger in them for him. Then he smiled wryly. 'I suppose I've no reason for saying that, except that the place looked deserted. I remember Tim saying, "Granny gone" and I suppose I just accepted it.'

He looked suitably embarrassed at this parental indulgence.

*

Bert Hook enjoyed the CID room. It was usually untidy, with men coming and going at irregular times when serious crime was afoot, as nowadays it invariably was. The room smelt of stale food and staler cigarette smoke; mugs half full of cold tea spoke of the urgent calls of modern detection.

But the place had an air of purpose, a certainty about the necessity of what the occupants were about, an agreement about the war on villains, which he knew in no other place. When there was a big hunt on—when a child had been killed, for instance—there was an atmosphere like the one people said they remembered from the war, when Hitler united a whole nation in the way in which this small specialist body of men were united now by crime.

DS Hook grumbled about his paper work and his unsocial hours like the rest, but he knew that even they were rituals he would miss if they were suddenly withdrawn from him. And he loved the banter, not realizing in his modest way how much he contributed to it, how much the collective spirit he loved was derived from long-serving men like him.

He looked for a moment at the application for a search warrant to investigate the living quarters of Everton Smith. They would get it easily enough; in the midst of a murder investigation, the sudden affluence which the black youth had refused to explain was sufficient reason to ascertain what other secrets he might be hiding in that mean little room he called home. It would be an invasion of the privacy the boy valued, but he had brought it upon himself.

Bert looked again at his notes on the interview at The Beeches and speculated uselessly upon Smith's refusal to account for the money he seemed to have acquired so suddenly. Could he be a drug-pusher? Many men of his background were small-time purveyors of pot and cocaine, drawn into the fringe of a sleazy world where they took the biggest risks and the anonymous men at the centre took practically none and made huge profits. Most small pushers were users themselves; Smith did not seem like one, though they had after all seen him only twice.

On his way home, Bert turned his Sierra on impulse towards the shabby street where Everton Smith guarded his small island of independence. They would have the search warrant tomorrow, but he would prefer that they did not have to use it. If he could have a quiet few words with the lad now, it might save Smith from not only loss of face but the loss of his accommodation. Landlords did not always like men who brought the police to their property, especially when they arrived with search warrants. Any rights possessed by men like Everton Smith tended to be strictly theoretical.

The high brick houses which had known so much better days rose high above Hook as he turned into Jackson Terrace, as if they were turning up their noses at the dubious vehicles which lined the street and the litter which gathered ever more thickly behind the unkempt privet hedges. Hook parked fifty yards from the house where Everton had his room; though he was in plain clothes, the expert eyes round here would soon spot a policeman.

He walked past two houses where the once proud bays at the front were boarded up, another where two vehicles were jacked up on the dank earth which had once been a bright front garden. He knocked at the front door of the house where Smith had his room. A thin young face peeped at him briefly through the filthy curtain to his left, then turned away so sharply that its pigtail brushed briefly against the window. Bert reflected that when he had begun his days in the force it had been curious, harmless old ladies who surveyed him thus. Now it was youth, usually with something to hide. Sometimes, in these days of drugs and knives and casual violence, dangerous youth.

The door opened three inches and the man with the pigtail looked through the gap with an automatic suspicion. He was a little older than Hook had thought: perhaps twenty-three or -four. His features, sharpened with the sly caution of his attitude, made him look older, but the acne and a couple of pink eruptions on his forehead spoke up defiantly for his disappearing youth. He did not speak.

Hook said, 'Police, son. Do you want to see the card?'

The face did not answer. Instead, it said, 'We paid the council tax. Or whatever fancy name you have for it now.'

'I don't doubt it, son.' Hook edged forward a little. He did not actually put his foot in the gap between the door and its frame, but he ensured that it would not now be slammed in his face. The gap widened from three to six inches. 'It's not you I want, lad. I want a few words with Everton Smith.'

'The wigwog on the first floor? What's he done, then?' It was the first curiosity the face had exhibited. It established that Smith would not receive assistance from this quarter, if he should need it.

'That would be telling, lad. Maybe nothing.' Hook's ample frame moved forward now, and the door fell open before its keeper quite realized what was happening. 'I know where his room is.' The burly guardian of the law glided past the man with the pigtail and ascended the staircase behind him with surprising speed and a minimum of noise. Like many big men, Hook made scarcely a sound as he climbed stairs, moving softly on the balls of his feel like a drunk trying to outwit a sleeping wife.

He rapped sharply at the scratched varnish on the dark door of Smith's room. When there was no reply, he turned the handle. The door was locked, of course: no man would leave his room open with residents like the man behind him around the place. But at least the locking probably meant that Smith was not here and not merely refusing to answer.

Hook went down the stairs. Pigtail waited to shepherd him safely on to the street and out of his life, but he turned abruptly by the baluster at the bottom of the stairs and went down the dark and narrow hall to the door at the end of it. It was the room where Lambert and he had sat and talked to Smith on their first visit to this place, before he took them up to his own room. The sink by the cracked window was still full of crockery, as if someone had arranged it carefully for a squalid still life painting. The bowl was half full of water, with grease congealing upon the surface. Hook assumed that they were not the same pots that had been there on his last visit, but it would have needed a very accurate observation to be sure of it.

The scratched table in the centre of the room was empty. There was no sign of Smith, nor of any possession of his. 'Do you know where he is?' he said to the man behind him, not even bothering to look round.

'No. Don't tell me where 'e's going or what 'e's doing, the wigwog don't.' Hook wondered if the man was trying to be offensive. Probably not; he sounded as if he might even be looking for common ground.

'I'm not surprised: I expect he has more sense.' Bert Hook was suddenly enraged. The speed of his movement again caught the youth off guard; the sergeant had the thin wrist in the grip of his large hand and the sleeve concertinaed up the arm before the man realized what was happening.

Both of them stared at the revealing pinpricks in the slug-white flesh. 'Supplies you with this, does he, the nignog?' said Hook.

The thin man felt very vulnerable in the face of this sudden rage. The white arm was stretched straight and slender between the two thick-fingered paws. It looked as though it could be broken like a stick if he provoked this strange creature with the village-bobby exterior and the unpredictability of a pitbull terrier. It was worse because he didn't know what had so incensed his captor. Was it the drugs or the words he had used to describe the black man? He said cautiously, 'No. Smith don't do drugs. Not his scene, that.'

Hook glared at him for a moment longer, their eyes no more than a foot apart. Then he relinquished the arm, slowly, as if he was tempted until the last instant to break it. 'What *is* his scene, lad?'

'I—I don't know.' Pigtail racked his brain, searching not for information but for any sort of answer which would satisfy his inquisitor. 'He's . . . well, a bit of a loner. Goes off to various jobs—I don't know what.'

'You wouldn't. He's hardly likely to confide in someone like you.' Hook turned in disgust and went across the dirty kitchen to the back door. He turned the knob on the Yale lock and went out into the yard, shutting the door on Pigtail without a backward glance. There was no one in the narrow yard. And no sign of the great white Honda motorcycle.

It was the moment when Hook felt for the first time that Everton Smith might be in some sort of danger.

## CHAPTER FIFTEEN

Lambert's way home led past the golf course. He thought of turning down the familiar lane and chancing that there might be someone available to play a few holes with him; now that the longer evenings were here, there were often other people like him around, seeking to unwind after a day's work.

But he realized when the moment of decision came that he was too tired; perhaps that was another sign that the years were catching up on him. But he knew he was wearied more by his failure to break this case than by the actual hours of work. Progress brought its own adrenalin, but there had not been much of that yet.

When he saw that the parking bay by a roadside viewpoint was quite empty, he turned into it on impulse and stopped his engine. It was part of his attempt to keep his work separate from his home, to do even his thinking about the problems of detection away from the house. It did not work, of course, as his wife knew better than he. When he was immersed in a case, it occupied all of his attention; it was the exclusion of any domestic consideration which had almost broken their marriage in the early days.

The setting sun threw an almost Italian ambience over a typically English scene, gilding it with old master colours. In this part of the country, there were still miles of hedgerows and stone walls stretching in irregular lines over the tracts of green farmland. In the distance the lazy bends of the Severn ran in their great silver curves, burning crimson only at the point where the low red sun reflected like fire from the water. The only movements he caught were from the corner of his golf course in the foreground; he could see four small figures moving like ants along the sixth fairway.

He thought of another golfer on another course, James Pritchard, and of the wife he had lost. This killing could hardly now be the random act of violence by a stranger, that sequence of events urged upon him by the members of the bereaved family. Now that it was established that the body had been moved from the house in the dead woman's own car, with no signs of a burglary, the overwhelming probability was that the murder was the work of a member of the family or a close acquaintance.

So far, Jim Pritchard was the only one who could not have done it—assuming, of course, that Everton Smith's assurance that the victim had been alive two days after her husband left for Spain was genuine. And even then Pritchard could have employed someone to remove his wife while he was so convincingly absent: contract killings were increasing each year, as Britain continued to import only the worst habits from across the Atlantic. It was statistically unlikely, perhaps; contract killers operated mostly for gangster bosses in the cities. But by no means impossible: Pritchard had the funds to arrange this method of dispatch, and he did not seem unduly distressed by his wife's death.

Mark Warner could certainly have done it. He had made no secret of his dislike for his mother-in-law, and his desperate need for funds to rescue his business gave him an obvious motive. And he had lied about his visit to The

Beeches on the Sunday after Jim Pritchard had gone to Spain. Lambert had not decided yet whether he believed the explanation Warner had now provided for the visit— that he had taken his toddler son in an attempt to loosen the heartstrings and pursestrings of Laura Pritchard at the same time. His story of finding the place locked and barred and his assertion that the dead woman had gone away hardly tallied with Everton Smith's story of working with the dead woman on the next day. Had Warner had some kind of exchange with Laura Pritchard which he was now trying to conceal? If so, the CID could hardly quiz the two-year-old who had been the only witness to the meeting.

He still found it curious that neither of the Warners had reported the dead woman's disappearance. It had seemed very odd at the time that the first report of a missing person should come not from the family but from the workplace, though they now knew that Sue Hendry had been much more than a colleague of Laura Pritchard.

He must have another word soon with Joyce Warner, that daughter who seemed so composed and ungrieving. He had the impression that she, like her husband, had been concealing something when he had seen her with Hook. Was she protecting her husband, or herself? Could she have killed her own mother? It was perfectly possible physically: the method by which wire or rope which had been twisted like a tourniquet into Laura Pritchard's slim neck needed no great strength. And ruthless violence among women was not as rare as men of Lambert's generation liked to suppose, especially where the interests of children or a cherished spouse were at stake.

Perhaps she was merely lying to protect that strange, rather pathetic younger brother of hers. If Peter Brooke had really been around at The Beeches as Everton Smith claimed on the Monday when the victim had last been alive, he became automatically a prime suspect, particularly as he had not admitted to that visit. He was the only one who had said openly that he had hated the victim, that he was glad she was dead. Whether with reason or not, he blamed his mother for the death of the father he had loved. From Rushton's detailed account of his interview with Brooke, he had a picture of a young man who was probably disturbed enough to be unbalanced. That was a common enough profile for family murderers; their degeneration into psychopathy was often not noticed until they had killed.

This was a strange family, with undercurrents he was sure they had not yet discovered. Not one of them seemed to be stricken with grief by this death, though sometimes the bereaved in a murder case exhibited a calm exterior to outsiders which was seen as a means of protecting their private suffering. All of them were significant financial beneficiaries of this death—even her husband was now the sole owner of his substantial house.

There were also two possibilities from outside the family. Everton Smith was an obvious suspect: from his edgy bearing under questioning, he even appeared to think so himself. By his own account, he was the last person known to have seen the victim alive. And he had acquired large sums of cash from somewhere at around the time of this death. Perhaps they should have pressed him harder about that, but Lambert had felt that the search warrant, giving them the opportunity to investigate his living quarters, might throw up much more than the answer to one question. Well, they would know more of Smith tomorrow, when the search warrant was agreed by the magistrates.

And there was a lover in this case. Lovers were always of interest: where there was love, other passions were rarely far away. Sue Hendry had given them the news of her relationship with the dead woman herself, when she might well have concealed it. She had produced it with a lover's pride and defiance. But could she have been rejected? Had the enigmatic Laura Pritchard proclaimed her intention to stay after all with her husband? It was often the moment of final commitment, in both homosexual and heterosexual relationships, which made the partner who was already in a marriage decide against the upheaval of a new life with the lover. They needed to know more of the determined and capable Sue Hendry.

The opportunity came to him sooner than he had expected. He ran the old Vauxhall into the garage and paused to examine the burgeoning buds of the roses on his way into the house. 'Home at last, Christine,' he called. He did not tell her that he had nearly called in at the golf club and been two hours later. Food was never spoiled in this house: Mrs Lambert had learned at least to protect herself from that over a quarter of a century of being married to the force.

She came to meet him at the back door of the house where she knew he would enter. She was trim and efficient in jeans and a sweat-shirt; her white trainers with their sky blue trimmings were bright against the dimmer light of the room behind her. 'You have a visitor, John,' she whispered. 'She insisted on waiting. I rang the CID section and they said you'd left for home.' Lambert breathed a sigh of relief to the golfing gods that he had not indulged himself on the fairways; even the patience of a saintly spouse had its limits.

He went through into the lounge. They had not yet put on the lights, and Sue Hendry's red hair glowed like a lamp in the twilit room. She stood up as he arrived in the room, his head almost brushing the door frame as it always did. She had on a grey skirt and a white blouse; her cardigan was over her wrist rather than around her shoulders; her court shoes had the medium heels which combine smartness with a degree of comfort. He divined that she, like him, had come here straight from work.

Perhaps not quite straight from work: maybe she—again like him—had paused to assess things. For he saw that she had been crying. Her eyes looked an even deeper green, because the puffing of the skin around them set them deeper in the cavities beneath the sandy eyebrows and the square forehead. She had stood up when she heard him coming into the room; now she moved with automatic grace towards the armchair to which he gestured. The contrast between the sturdy athleticism of her movements and her emotional uncertainty was peculiarly poignant: hockey-playing women should be jolly and uncomplicated.

Sue Hendry was no longer a girl: in her distress, her forty years showed up as they often did not. She had expected this tall man with the experienced face and the grey-flecked hair to speak first in his own house. When he said nothing she said automatically, 'I—I'm sorry for coming here. To your house, I mean. I shouldn't have done that. I realize it now.'

'Who gave you this address?' His first reaction had been that of annoyance; already he could feel curiosity overriding it as the instincts of the crime-hunter asserted themselves.

'You gave me your name when you came to the office. My receptionist thought she had been to a WEA history class taught by your wife; she remembered that the tutor's husband was a senior policeman and the village where she lived. I took a chance and rang. A bit of detective work, you might say.' She tried to twist his tail with a laugh at his expense, but it turned without warning into a breathless little sob.

It must have been over ten years since that class: Christine had left an impression, as usual. He fought down the pride in her that he knew was irrelevant to this. 'But she didn't invite you here.' He knew his wife never did that.

'No. She confirmed that this was your home, that's all. And when I came, she didn't turn me away but put me in here and offered me a cup of tea. I'm grateful to her for that.'

He said stiffly, 'And why did you think it necessary to come here, Miss Hendry? You could have gone to the station at Oldford, or I would have come to see you again at your office or your home.' It was the last piece of a ritual protest, a concession to the part of him that said his home was sacrosanct. He would delay their business no longer.

'I was frightened. Someone killed Laura. At first that was all I could think of; my grief stopped me from thinking it through. Now I think that they might kill me.' She delivered the melodramatic phrases as though they were a grocery list, as though the perfect logic of her argument must be obvious to anyone who heard it.

Lambert thought it unlikely that she was in danger, but he did not dismiss the idea out of hand. Fear was the most potent weapon he had to prise information from people. An ordinary member of the public would immediately have tried to reassure a distressed woman; he sought to use her apprehension as a tool. 'Do you think the person who killed Mrs Pritchard hates you?'

She shook her head, puzzled that he should even suggest it. 'No. Why should he?'

Lambert could think of a reason, but he did not suggest it. 'And do you think he—you seem to be assuming that our killer is a man—has anything material to gain from your death?'

'No. Of course not.'

'Then you can only be in danger if he sees you as a threat to him. If you have some special piece of knowledge about him. Something you have so far not revealed to us.'

If she noticed the rebuke in that, it did not register in her features. She was watching him with her head a little on one side, like a trusting schoolgirl; she reminded him in that moment of his own daughters when they were no more than eight or nine. She took in a long breath, its evenness disturbed by the emotion that was still lurking where she thought she had got it under control. 'There are—things which might be significant. Things I've only thought about since I saw you. I was still coming to terms with the fact that Laura had been murdered then. It's—it's been a great shock to me, you see.'

Now, when she least wanted it, the tears began to flow again. She pulled a handkerchief from the black bag at her side and bludgeoned her face with it, angry that this weakness should assert itself when she was so anxious to be calm and lucid. Lambert walked across to the corner cupboard and took out a whisky bottle and a glass. He poured her a stiff measure and she shook her head, then reached for it tentatively as he urged it wordlessly upon her. She gulped at it in a way which proved that she was no spirit drinker; coughed; pulled a medicinal face; felt the comfort of the warm fire as it ran through her throat.

Lambert said nothing, knowing that she wanted to speak, was striving only for control. Eventually she said, 'I broke down when you saw me in the office, as well. You must think I do nothing but cry. That I'm a stupid, emotional little woman.'

He said, 'Certainly not stupid. And we all have our emotions. For what it's worth, I've seen men cry, much more often than you would think. Tears are nothing to be ashamed of.'

She looked up at him to see if he was patronizing her, then nodded twice. 'I told you Laura and I were lovers, that we had been so for almost two years. You were well enough trained not to look astonished, for which I thank you. Well, there was a little more to it than that. We were supposed to be going away together for a few days during the time while Jim Pritchard was away in Spain.'

Lambert nodded, remembering the notes for the cleaner, the cancelling of the milk. This seemed to establish not only that those directions from the dead woman were genuine, but the nature of the trip she had proposed during that week. 'What day were you going away together?'

'Tuesday. We needed to spend Monday in the office to make sure everything was set up smoothly for the week. We'd been away together before when the opportunity arose.'

'How many times?'

She looked momentarily annoyed at this prying into her affairs; then she accepted that it was not mere prurience. 'Four or five. All of them in the last year. There was a difference this time. When Jim Pritchard came home, Laura was going to tell him that she was leaving.'

'Did he know about your affair?'

'It was more than an affair, Superintendent.' She was defending all she had left of what had meant so much to her. 'He knew about our relationship, yes. Laura was too honest to conceal such things for very long. It—it took her a while to come to terms with her own sexuality. I was the first and the only woman that she loved, you see.'

Her pride in that was pathetic, much more touching than it would have been had the sentiment come from a teenager. Nothing makes us so vulnerable as love, he thought.

'Who else in the family knew of the—relationship?'

This time it was he who had hesitated for a word, and she acknowledged the fact with a bleak little smile. 'No one else, as far as I know. I don't know whether Jim Pritchard kept the knowledge to himself, of course—Laura said he was so outraged that he would be too ashamed to tell anyone, but I don't know that he didn't. And I don't know whether any of them found out after I'd last seen Laura on that Friday, do I?'

'Do you think she was in contact with her children in the days before her death?' He wondered how much she knew of the puzzling Joyce Warner and Peter Brooke.

She nodded. 'She didn't leave me in the office on that Friday afternoon, as I told you when you came to see me. I went back to the house with her. Jim had her Astra, because his Jaguar was being serviced, so I dropped her off. It was the last time I saw her.' He expected that recollection to fracture her precarious composure, but she was full of the fact she wanted to give him. 'As I was driving away, I saw Peter Brooke walking up the lane.'

'You know him?'

'I've seen him once, at a distance. I've also seen pictures of him. And he had his violin case in his hand.'

It was almost Brooke's trademark, that case. Two people had identified him by it now. If he had been around The

Beeches on both the Friday and then again on the Monday, as Everton Smith claimed, he had some explaining to do. Especially as he had denied being near the place for weeks.

'What do you know about him?'

'Only that he bitterly resented the break-up of Laura's first marriage. She said he blamed her for his father's physical decline and death after she left. Laura was fond of him, but she never found it easy to show her deeper feelings, even to her children. She wanted to help him, but he wouldn't believe that. I think she was hoping he would complete his music course and look for a job with a symphony orchestra. That had always been his ambition, you see.'

'Was she expecting him on that Friday?'

'No. I'm sure she wasn't. She'd have mentioned it to me.'

'Presumably he saw his mother. Do you know how long he was at The Beeches?'

'No. I thought of ringing that night, but I was afraid of Jim answering the phone. That would have been too embarrassing. I rang again on the Saturday evening, after he had gone off abroad, but there was no reply.'

'How many times did you ring?'

The square brow puckered; a line of concentration furrowed the space between the sandy eyebrows. She was conjecturing about the purpose of his question rather than the answer to it. 'Twice. At seven o'clock and nine-forty.' Only a lover would remember so precisely those attempted contacts.

'So you concluded no doubt that she was out. Do you know of any friends that she might have been visiting? We're trying to piece together a picture of her movements in those last days, but we haven't had a great deal of success so far.' He saw no need to tell her of Everton Smith's having seen the dead woman alive and apparently normal on the Monday after this—at present their latest reported sighting.

'No. She had friends, of course. She kept up with some of the people from the choir, for instance, although she no longer sang with them. But I think she would have told me if she had been planning to visit them on the Saturday. We didn't have secrets from each other, you see.'

She spoke again with the shy pride of passion; Lambert had seen such views shattered hundreds of times, seen the most appalling deceptions and betrayals of people who had shown similar trust. But there was no point in telling her that; nor that their inquiries had also shown that none of her friends among the choir had been in contact with Laura Pritchard in the last month of her life. He said, 'Did you make any attempt to contact her on the Sunday?'

'Yes. I rang again on the Sunday morning. When there was no reply, I drove round to The Beeches—I was getting anxious by this time, you see.'

'And did you find her?'

'No. The place was locked and barred.' Exactly the same phrase that Mark Warner had used, he recalled. She looked desperately miserable. 'I've thought about it a lot since. Perhaps Laura was lying dead inside.' A small tear dropped suddenly on to the back of her hand: she looked at it sadly, as though it had come too late to join its fellows. There was no sob this time.

Lambert found her infinitely moving. With no sexual complication between them to weaken his judgement, none of his automatic caution against a pretty face, he felt a huge pity for her suffering, her isolation, her determination that the killer of her lover should be brought to justice, whatever the cost to her privacy. He almost told her that Smith had seen Laura Pritchard alive and cheerful on the Monday. Then he reminded himself sternly that this resolute red-haired creature might after all be a murderer. There was no call to give her information which might be useful.

Instead he said, 'I think it most unlikely that she was in the house at that time. It is overwhelmingly probable that her killer took the body to the river immediately after she died.' He did not tell her that Laura Pritchard had almost certainly died at her own house; nor did he torment her with the details of rigor mortis and the difficulties of transferring a corpse which had stiffened.

She did not find much consolation in his statement, but he had not expected her to. She looked him full in the face for a moment, her green eyes glistening with tears in their puffed-up sockets; then she said, 'Do you think she was dead by then?'

'If she was, someone is lying. Did you try all the doors?'

'Yes. I walked right round the house. I peered in at the downstairs windows. I told you: I was worried about Laura by then.'

'Did you see any sort of note left around?'

'Note?' She looked as blank as if he had made some deeply mysterious suggestion.

'Yes. You said she was planning to go away with you. We know that she cancelled the milk and told her cleaning lady that she would be away. I wondered if the notes which she wrote were visible to you on the Sunday. Under a stone, perhaps, near the front or the back door?'

She thought for a moment. 'No. There was nothing there. I'm sure I'd have seen it, because I was anxious for any sign of her by then. But we weren't going until the Tuesday, so she wouldn't have put a note out so early, would she?'

'Probably not.' He hoped she would not work out the possibility that her lover might have changed her mind and gone away earlier to avoid her; even if she regarded that as impossible, it was something the police had to take into account. If she was speaking the truth now, it meant that Laura Pritchard had probably been alive after that Sunday, as Everton Smith had told them. He looked at her face, tear-stained and emotionally exhausted, but still earnest with information. She had something more to tell him yet.

He said, 'What did you do after you had walked round the house?'

'I sat for ten minutes in my car on the drive, wondering

where she could be, hoping against hope that she would come back while I was there. Then I drove away. As I went through the village, I saw Laura's son-in-law. He passed me in his car.'

'Mark Warner. Was there anyone with him?'

'I didn't see anyone. But he was almost past me before I realized it was him. I haven't seen him for years, except in photographs Laura had of her grandchildren. But he used our agency to get temporary staff, when his business was doing better.'

Lambert nodded. It was possible, even probable, that she could have missed a toddler in the back of the car. That was almost Warner's guarantee of good intent, though it was still possible that he had used his son to cover some more malicious purpose. 'What did you do then?'

'I parked by the village church: there were several other vehicles there. I knew that Laura didn't like her son-in-law, and by this time I was very worried about her. I was there about half an hour—perhaps a little less than that, if anything. Then Mark Warner came back.'

'Did he see you?'

'No. I doubt whether he'd have recognized me, anyway, but I was parked on the other side of the green. He drove straight along the road and out of the village.'

'Still alone?'

'Yes. As far as I'm aware. I wasn't looking for anyone else.'

'Did you follow him?'

'No. There was no reason why I should.'

'Of course not.' But the road he had taken could have led to the river, as well as towards his home. It was not impossible that he had picked up the body from the house, despite the reassurance Lambert had tried to give to Sue Hendry. But it would have meant that Everton Smith as well as Warner would have to be lying; they seemed an unlikely partnership. He said, 'You didn't see anything more of Peter Brooke on that Sunday?'

'No. I must admit he was in my mind, after I'd seen him on the Friday. But I didn't find any trace of him, either around the house or in the village. I went into the pub on the green. It was full of locals and I listened to the gossip, but I didn't hear anything which seemed significant.'

He said, 'You might make a good detective with a little training,' and the square open face lit up for a moment with a grin which showed the lively woman she must be in more normal circumstances.

She refused the offer of police protection, saying she felt safer for having talked to him. He saw her off the premises, but she insisted on calling her thanks through to the discreetly absent Christine. She paused for a moment after she had buckled on her car safety belt, looking up at him; then she said with fierce intensity, 'You must get the one who killed Laura, John Lambert. And keep him away from me, when you do!' Then she drove away without another look at him or the house.

He stood looking after the car in the near-darkness. The evening was so still that he could hear its high-revving engine for almost a mile. Then he went back into the house, reflecting on what his visitor had said, determined to be objective in his assessments. He reminded himself again that it was Sue Hendry who had first reported the disappearance of Laura Pritchard.

But that was not until later in the week, when the body had been in the Severn for some time and the trail was already cold.

## CHAPTER SIXTEEN

Joe Brooking was that rare animal, a farmer satisfied with the weather. Perhaps he should have been stuffed and mounted and set in some museum of agricultural curiosities.

After a wet April, the long days of sun were just what was needed for the eight-acre meadow and the pasture fields which sloped gently down to the river. If such days continued for another week, he would be looking anxiously at the skies and shaking his head with his fellows, but for the moment he acknowledged that the elements were behaving with unusual complicity.

Now there was a lull in the hectic progress of his year. Townsmen did not think of late spring as a slack time for farmers, because they thought in terms of gardens, not farming: he permitted himself a superior smile at the thought of such urban naïvety. After the year's hectic early months of lambing, these weeks felt like a holiday to Joe. The sheep and the cattle were out to pasture, and the pasture this year was good; the weeks in late autumn when the Severn had climbed its banks and turned six acres of his fields into a shallow lake seemed but a distant memory as the offending river flowed placidly within its emerald confines.

Soon there would be sheep to shear, and a little while later the hay to cut, but for the moment there was a lull in the pace, on this particular farm, at least. It was a good time for mending fences; good fences were supposed to make good neighbours, according to one of the poets of Joe Brooking's youth. He was on his way to inspect the northern boundaries of his property, the point furthest away from the long low house of Cotswold stone which was the centre of his green little corner of industry. But he had time to pause for a moment to lean on the gate between two of his fields: when he was unobserved, Joe still liked to indulge the joy of possession: he had worked for twenty years to get his own farm.

Those town-dwellers who are silly enough to think themselves superior to countrymen have fixed images of the people they expect to find in a rural landscape. They would have appreciated the image of the rustic leaning on his gate, composed by *Punch* a century earlier, which now outlives the magazine which created it. But Joe Brooking was no yokel. He could have given you a few more lines of Robert Frost if you had pressed him, and he had read his Thomas Hardy, as well as factual histories of the long nineteenth-century agricultural depression which those novels took as a background.

And he could read a landscape. From this highest point of his kingdom, near to the buzzard which had wheeled intermittently over his head for the last two months, there was history apparent for those who knew where to look for it. Joe's was not by modern standards a large farm, but it was still the result of an amalgamation between four smaller units. Joe mused as he had before on the harsh lives of those who had tried so hard and so hopelessly to wring a living from tracts so small, so uneconomic. That was one of his agricultural college words, which those desperate scratchers after a livelihood would not even have understood.

He looked towards the hovel, no more than a hundred feet from the river, where one of those anonymous sufferers had lived. His land could have been little bigger than a modern smallholding, sandwiched on uneven ground between the river and the lane, which bent towards it here as if deliberately to squeeze the land into a narrow strait. Only the foundations of what had once been a home remained, the stones having been removed to repair walls elsewhere on the enlarged farm. But beside these there stood what had once been a small barn, still with half its roof intact. Joe's predecessor had stored machinery in it for a while thirty years earlier, until the cost of repairs outweighed this marginal usefulness and he had left it to decay.

As Joe Brooking looked at that shattered building and mused on the hard, unlamented days it had seen, he caught a glimpse of something white behind it, among the straggling hawthorns which had once been a hedge. Had those buggers with their cars and vans been using his land as a dumping ground again? He had cleared a mattress, a bedstead, a bicycle wheel, even the casing of an old twin-tub washing machine from the ditch a little further down the lane only a month earlier. Now it seemed that they were even invading his land. The barn was almost on his route to the fence he wanted to inspect. He went down the slope of the hillside to investigate.

Where the track from the road ran under the shade of an oak, the ground was still soft enough for him to see tyre marks in the clay surface. Some vehicle had travelled along here, and recently; his anger quickened. The old barn still had half a roof, but there were holes where tiles had cracked and fallen. The wind which had been a pleasant breeze when he leaned upon the gate was colder and stronger here, sweeping along the side of the valley, whining in the ruined rafters like a live thing in search of comfort.

As he came up beside the hole in the barn which had once been a door, he heard another sound. A tapping—irregular but insistent—as if something was being moved by the wind and touching some obstruction. Surely the intruders hadn't dumped stuff in here? He turned abruptly to his right and went into the barn.

There was nothing apparent in the first section. Ahead of him was an internal wall which was almost in its original condition, having at once supported and been protected by the best remaining part of the roof. The tapping came from somewhere on the other side of it. When he went beyond the wall, he saw at first only the heap of wooden detritus which had been here for years: rotting rafters which had fallen, some worm-eaten floorboards from the house which had once adjoined the barn, an old panelled door with its green paint all but gone.

Then he lifted his eyes from the floor and saw what it was that was making that slight but persistent noise. The heels of black boots, a good two feet above the damp ground, swung gently backwards and forwards, tapping gently against the panel of that long abandoned door, as if demanding entry.

But any entry granted would be in the next world, not this. Joe Brooking's eyes travelled upwards, over the slim legs, the hands which hung limp and lifeless in front of the hips, the waist which was trim even beneath the thick leathers, to the point where the rope bit deeply into the thin young neck and cruelly distorted the neat black features of the face above it.

Joe Brooking had seen plenty of death, but he looked away quickly from the bulbous desperation of these eyes. In the last convulsions before death, an envelope had come half out of the side pocket of the hanged man. Brooking reached up gingerly and removed it. It was a standard letter from the DVLC at Swansea, reminding the addressee that his road tax would shortly be due.

It was addressed to a Mr Everton Smith.

## CHAPTER SEVENTEEN

The narrow lane had not been designed for motor vehicles. There was scarcely room for the police Rover and the 'death wagon' in the space by the entrance to the field; Lambert parked the old Vauxhall further down the road, with its passenger door hard against the hedge. Hook had to scramble awkwardly across the gear lever and the driver's seat to join him on the lane.

It was two hours now since Joe Brooking had phoned in the news of Everton Smith's death. The police surgeon had been and gone, spending no more than five minutes over his certification of the formalities of death. As they approached the gate to the field, where fluttering plastic ribbons fenced off the area from the non-existent public, the corpse in its fibreglass 'shell' was being carefully eased into the plain van for its journey to the pathologist's post-mortem table. Bert Hook wondered glumly what next of kin could be dredged up to identify the youth whose father was dead and whose mother had long ago deserted him.

A grim-faced Lambert paused for a moment at the gate to take in the scene of this second death. The Severn moved so slowly here that it might almost have been a lake; the peaceful green pastures ran away on the other side of it towards the Malvern Hills. The landscape which had inspired Elgar seemed a curious backdrop to their business here. The superintendent turned his attention to the more pressing human matters in the foreground of the scene. A hundred yards in front of him, four officers had already begun the detailed searching of the ground around the tumbledown barn where all that remained of Everton Smith had been discovered.

The men kept their heads down as the chief approached with Hook, both of them treading warily on the grass beside the unpaved track so as to make sure they did not confuse any evidence that route might offer. Behind them, they heard the patient tones of the uniformed officer explaining to the 'death wagon' driver why he had not been able to allow a vehicle to go down to the barn itself to retrieve the mortal remains of the hanged man.

The method of death was the first thing to check. Sergeant 'Jack' Johnson, the SOC officer, took one look at Lambert's face and decided that this was a morning to be carefully factual and concise. 'He hanged all right,' he said, in answer to the superintendent's first grunted query. 'The doctor talked about cerebral anaemia and inhibition as well as asphyxiation, but he had no doubt that the lad died by hanging from that beam.'

So the first question which had insinuated its way into devious CID minds—that of whether the man might have been killed elsewhere and strung up here in a crude attempt at deception—was answered. They looked up at the huge transom which ran from the outer to the inner wall of the barn, almost the only sound timber left in the building, it seemed. The rope which had killed Smith hung in a sinister halter from the beam, looking like the instrument of retribution which the law of the kingdom had once brought to convicted killers.

Perhaps it was that thought which made Johnson say rather nervously, 'It looks at the moment as if the black lad was overcome by remorse, sir. As if he killed Laura Pritchard and then came back here to kill himself when he felt you were close to arresting him.'

'Back here?' said Hook.

'Yes. It seems as if we've finally found the place where Laura Pritchard's body was dumped in the river.' Johnson led them outside and took a single photocopied sheet from the folder in his case. 'When forensic were able to tell us that the body had been taken to the Severn in the victim's own car, we took photographs of the tyre treads to compare with anything we found near the river. There are far too many points of access over the ten miles or so where we're told the body was most probably put in the river. It's been like looking for a needle in a haystack, but it looks as if Smith has led us back to the place he used.'

'You've found tracks from Laura Pritchard's car here?' said Lambert.

'I'm almost sure of it. We'll compare soil samples with those we took from the tyre treads to confirm it, but I'm already certain in my own mind.' Johnson led the way down to the point five yards from the edge of the river where the firm grass ended and bare earth dropped more abruptly towards the water. At the place where the two surfaces met, there was a six-inch long tyre tread mark, not new, but still clear enough in this quiet place to be compared with the picture in Johnson's hand.

They looked for a moment at the long reach of the river that stretched away downstream, picturing the indistinct figure labouring under its macabre burden—the disposal must surely have taken place under the cover of darkness—the hurried attempts to weight the body, the eventual escape of the corpse from its restraints, and its slow progress downstream to the point where it had been retrieved. Hook said in a voice of infinite, unpolicemanly regret, 'I never thought it would have been young Smith.'

Lambert looked sharply at the two faces alongside him, then turned his back on the river and walked back towards the barn. The Honda 750, of which Everton Smith had been so proud, was upright again on its stand; it had taken the strenuous efforts of three men to retrieve it from the shallow ditch where it had lain partially hidden. It had taken some time, because they had fingerprinted the machine in situ before attempting to move it. There was a long scratch along the petrol tank where it had fallen upon a stone, cutting across the maker's lettering. Smith's delight in the machine meant that the damage leapt out at them like an accusation.

Lambert said, 'Had the bike been put under those hawthorns deliberately?'

The young PC who stood panting beside the handlebars glanced at his fellows and then said, 'Yes, sir, I'd say it must have been. If it had just fallen over off its stand, it couldn't have ended up down there.' He picked a twig out of his hair and stared at the bike, as if it was deliberately withholding information from him. 'I suppose he pushed it in there because he didn't want anyone to see it and come to see what was happening—wanted a bit of privacy for his last moments.'

Hook said, 'It's possible, I suppose. But he was very proud of that bike; his instinct would have been to protect it.' He ran his fingers gently over that livid scratch in the white cellulose.

Johnson, sensing what his fellow sergeant wanted to think, said gently, 'People about to commit suicide cease to be rational, Bert. And he knew he'd have no further use for the bike.'

'Did he leave a note?' asked Lambert.

'No, sir. Not here, at least; we haven't searched his

lodgings yet.' They all knew the significance of the question. Suicides usually left a note of some kind to explain their thinking, except on those rare occasions when the deed was a sudden impulse. It was an instinct to write a last, dramatic message in the book they were closing forever. Death gives even the meanest of lives the centre of the stage for a few short hours.

Lambert led the way back into the barn and surveyed the ground beneath the halter. 'What did he stand on, Jack?'

Johnson said, 'We haven't looked at it in detail yet, but it looks as if he made a platform out of those blocks of wood and planks there. You can see that it would have collapsed like that as he kicked it away.'

Lambert looked hard for a moment at the collection of broken and rotting timber, bending to look at two or three of the surfaces, but refraining from touching them. 'Better get this lot fingerprinted with the rest. If he made himself a platform, there should be plenty of his dabs around. And those boots he was wearing would probably have left some trace, if he stood on this lot and then kicked it away.'

He went outside and looked up and down the eighty yards of unpaved track which led up to the gate and the lane. 'You did well to keep your vehicles out on the road, Jack. Have you found any traces of other vehicles than Laura Pritchard's Astra and Smith's motorbike?'

'No, sir.' Smith tried not to look too pleased in the face of Lambert's approval of his methods; some of the officers within earshot had cursed him when they had been forced to carry the corpse up those hundred uneven yards to the van at the gate of the field. 'There are marks from the farmer's tractor, crossing this track at right angles just up there, but I'd be pretty confident that the bike and the Astra are the only two vehicles that have been down here in the last couple of months.'

Lambert nodded. 'Extend the search. Look around the place near the gate, where your car is and the van that collected the body was parked. If you don't find anything there, try the passing places further down the lane, including the spot where my own car is parked at the moment.'

Johnson looked abashed at the widening boundaries of the search area. He said, 'There are certain to have been other vehicles down there over the weeks. Even on a quiet lane like that there's—'

'Ignore any traces except the most recent. You're only looking for a vehicle that stood there for a little while last night. I don't think Everton Smith came here on his own.'

Joyce Warner had been expecting Lambert. She was glad that he came when her husband was at home. She had a feeling that she was going to need all the support she could muster.

Both of them stood for a moment like self-conscious teenagers when the two large CID men came unsmiling into their lounge. Lambert hesitated a moment when invited to sit down, then nodded curtly and sat with Hook on the sofa; he refused an offer of refreshment. He would rather have seen Joyce Warner without her husband, if only because they might be trapped into contradictions when interviewed separately, but he was well aware that there was nothing he could do about that. Both the people who now seated themselves gingerly in the armchairs to face him were cooperating voluntarily with police investigating a crime.

Lambert said without preamble, 'Can you tell us where your brother is, Mrs Warner?'

Joyce Warner swallowed hard, forcing her voice to be steady as she said, 'In London, as far as I know.'

'And where was he last night?'

'I really don't know. I'm not his keeper, you know: he's twenty-eight now.' She had meant it to be aggressive, an announcement that she was not going to be pushed around, but her voice quavered and it emerged almost as an apology. 'What happened last night?'

Lambert ignored the question. 'We shall need to pick him up for questioning. I should warn you that if you know his whereabouts and are choosing to conceal it, you could be charged with impeding the police in the course of an inquiry.'

He was hard-faced, urgent, demanding their assistance where once he had asked for it. 'I have reason to think that you concealed information from us about your brother, Mrs Warner. That he has in fact been in the area much more recently than you led us to believe.'

'What makes you think that Peter—'

'Did you in fact know that Peter Brooke visited The Beeches on the Friday before your mother's death? That he may well be the last person known to have seen her alive?'

She looked at her husband. 'It's all right, Mark. I didn't tell you because I felt that there was no point in your knowing. It would only have meant that two of us . . .' She stopped, aware that her anxiety to explain herself to her husband had led her into an admission.

It was Lambert who completed her sentence. '. . . That two of you were telling lies instead of one. Concealing information from those anxious to arrest your mother's killer.'

'It's just that Peter—'

'And now there has been another death.'

Both eyes widened in the faces opposite him; if one or both of them knew about this second death, they gave nothing away in their countenances. It was Mark Warner who said, 'Another death? But who—'

'I ask you again: do either of you know where Peter Brooke was last night?' They looked at each other, fear and confusion flitting across their faces; perhaps it was not such a bad idea to see them together after all. Lambert said, 'I advise you to consider your answers very seriously.'

It was Mark Warner who said quietly, 'I have no idea where Peter was last night.' They noticed that 'I', and the way he looked expectantly at his wife, sitting bolt upright now in the armchair beside him. The news that his wife knew that Peter had been in the area and had concealed the fact from him had driven a wedge between them, for the moment anyway.

Hook, taking his cue from this, looked up from his notebook to say, 'And what about you, Mrs Warner?'

Joyce Warner, staring straight ahead, said evenly, 'I have no idea where Peter was last night.'

Hook waited a moment to see if she would enlarge on this before he said, 'When did you last see your brother?'

'Two days ago. I met him in Gloucester Cathedral.'

'For what purpose?'

She glanced at her husband, then at the two relentless faces opposite her. 'Surely that is our own business.'

Lambert said harshly, impatiently, 'Surely you must see that it is ours now.'

Joyce Warner glanced again at Mark before she said in a low voice, 'Peter was scared. He thought you were going to arrest him for killing his mother. He hated her, you know, and he'd made no secret of the fact. He still blames her for Dad's death: I've tried to tell him that isn't fair but he won't listen. And he—he thought you'd find out about Mandy.'

Lambert gave nothing away in his lean features. 'You'd better tell us about her.'

'She was a National Youth Orchestra player at the same time as Peter. She went to the Northern College of Music when Peter was at the Royal College, but they kept in touch. Peter came home and said they were getting engaged and Mother went up the wall. I don't know what she had against Mandy, who was a nice, rather serious girl. Perhaps she was just too pretty. But it's not as though Peter had ever been particularly a mother's boy—he was always much closer to Dad, and Mum had been quite happy to have it that way, as far as I could see.'

Lambert would normally have let her run on, anxious to find as much as possible of the relationship between a murder victim and a leading suspect. But the second killing had given an extra edge of urgency and he said testily, 'What happened to the girl?'

'Mum was awful to her. When she'd gone, she said she wouldn't have her in the house again. It was ridiculous, because she was pleasant and friendly to my parents—you couldn't imagine anyone more inoffensive. Peter was still very taken with her, but Mum wrote to her a few months later. We never found out quite what she said, but Mandy and Peter broke up shortly afterwards.'

'And that was the end of the matter?'

'No. Peter and Mandy were still very young, and it's my belief that they would have got together again once they had finished their courses and found their feet in the world: I think they even felt that themselves. But Dad died and Peter chucked up his course. Mandy qualified well, but she didn't get job offers immediately: it isn't always easy for viola players. She went off to India on a nursing project for a year—apparently that was something she'd always wanted to do.'

'And did she take up things with your brother again when she came back?'

Again there was a glance between husband and wife. This time it was Mark Warner who said in a low voice, 'She didn't come back, Superintendent. She died from cholera when she was out there.'

'Leaving Peter Brooke with another reason to hate his mother?'

Joyce opened her mouth to deny it, but Mark reached across and put his hand upon her forearm. He said gently, 'You've done everything you can for him, dear. If he did kill her, he needs help.' Turning his face back to Lambert, he nodded. 'Peter was devastated. In my view, it's one reason why he dropped out completely and has been living as he has. He certainly blamed Laura for what happened to Mandy—with some reason, I must say. That doesn't mean he killed his mother, though.'

'Indeed it doesn't. But it gives him an even stronger motive. And that in turn makes it even more important that we have details of his movements, both at the time of his mother's death and last night. Tell me about this meeting you had with him two days ago.'

'He rang me up because he was scared. He sounded very strange. You—you must understand that he has a very odd lifestyle in London, and that we really know very little about it. I'm closer to him than anyone: I used to be very close; when he was small, I was more a substitute mother than an elder sister. Then he deliberately isolated himself from my life here, after Dad and Mandy had died. It's only over these last two years that we've been getting closer again.' She looked across at her husband, who gave her a small, encouraging smile and withdrew his hand from her arm. 'We've been hoping he'd get back on the rails, that he'd finish his course and get a job with an orchestra. He could, you know, even with the competition as fierce as it is now: he's a brilliant violinist.' Her pride in her brother flashed out: for a moment it was more important that she convinced them of his virtuosity than his innocence.

'What happened when you met him in Gloucester?'

'We went to the cathedral. We met by the tomb of Edward II. Then we sat in the Lady Chapel and talked for quite a long time. I was trying to convince him that he should contact the Royal College of Music, as he'd agreed to do before this happened. He wouldn't be eligible for a grant any more, but Mum had more or less agreed that she would support him. The only condition was that he should see her and make his peace. As far as I know, he didn't manage to do that.'

'Not even when he saw her on the Monday before he died?' Lambert threw in Everton Smith's statement as a fact; whether it was true or not, the boy was never going to have the opportunity to change it now.

Joyce Warner's eyes widened in something near horror. 'If Peter was there then, he never told me about it.'

'Not even when you talked to him in Gloucester?'

'No.' Her face was bleak and pinched; perhaps she was contemplating for the first time the fact that the younger brother she had protected was a murderer. Or perhaps, Hook reminded himself as he returned his eyes assiduously to his notebook, she was now protecting her husband or herself.

'How long was he with you?'

'Two hours; perhaps two and a half; no more. I had to get back to collect Katie from nursery school. I wanted him to come back here with me but he wouldn't: he said he must get back to London. We had some tea in a little café before we went our separate ways.'

'And did you see him on to his train?' When she hesitated, he said sharply, 'Lies will be no use to him and could easily land you in a lot of trouble, Mrs Warner.'

For a moment she glared at him so resentfully that he thought she was going to shout. Then she accepted the logic of his warning and said with an air of hopelessness, 'No. He didn't go towards the station when we left the café, he turned in the other direction. I thought he was making for the ring road, planning to hitch back to London: he's done that quite often before.'

Lambert pressed remorselessly: he had no sympathy for a woman who had deceived him once. 'So in fact we have no real assurance at this moment that he left the area at all. I suggest that in your own interests you now take the greatest care to answer my next question as honestly and fully as you can. To your knowledge, when was the last occasion when Peter Brooke contacted his mother?'

The small, neat face tightened with concentration in its frame of blue-black hair. Her forehead wrinkled in that characteristic symbol of the mental activity behind it. For a moment she looked like an earnest schoolgirl, doing her best to remember the lines of a poem or a detail of history. When she spoke, it was as if she was delivering just such a careful recapitulation. 'I did deceive you when I saw you earlier in the week, Mr Lambert. It was in an attempt to protect Peter. Not because I think him capable of killing anyone, but because I thought his recovery to a normal life was at risk. I recognize now that the attempt was mistaken. Peter last went to see my mother on the Friday afternoon before she died. If he saw her three days later than that as you say, I am not aware of it; he did not mention any such meeting when I saw him in Gloucester on Monday.'

In another room, Tim was waking from his daytime nap; the burblings of the two-year-old came to them clearly in the still house—an innocent reminder that Joyce Warner had responsibilities to others as well as her brother. Mark Warner, reinforcing this impression, said, 'Who was it who told you that Peter was at The Beeches on that Monday two weeks earlier, Superintendent?'

Lambert watched both their faces as he said, 'It was Everton Smith, who did gardening work for Laura Pritchard.'

There was a pause. Then Joyce, tight-lipped and strained, said, 'I know him: the black boy. I think he's lying.'

Lambert said, 'Well, we shall find out when we talk to Peter, won't we? You can see why it's in his interests to clear himself, if he's as innocent as you say.'

Mark said, 'What Joyce said is that she doesn't think he was there on that Monday two weeks ago, that's all.' He seemed to be trying to distance them from Peter Brooke, as if he had decided now from his more objective standpoint that he might be a killer. Then he said, as if the possibility was occurring as a pleasant surprise to him, 'Isn't it quite likely that Smith is not only lying but also the killer of my mother-in-law? Have you grilled him about that Monday in the way you propose to grill Peter?'

Joyce looked at him, a little flush of gratitude colouring her white face for the first time in these exchanges. If they knew about this second death, neither of them had put a foot wrong in projecting their ignorance of it. Lambert said quietly, 'We should very much like to question Everton Smith, Mr Warner. Unfortunately, we cannot interrogate a dead man.'

Whatever they knew about the facts of this death, their reaction to the news of it was perfect, from the quick gasps of surprise to the fear which followed upon their faces. It was Joyce Warner, speaking as if the question was wrung from an unwilling throat, who said in a voice not much above a whisper, 'How did he die?'

'He was found hanging from a beam in a remote barn. Not more than fifty yards from the spot where Laura Pritchard's weighted body was put into the Severn. He died last night.' There was a long silence, punctuated bizarrely by the increasingly insistent infant burblings from beyond the wall. Lambert and Hook were old hands at this game, prepared to exploit the tenseness that hung like a tangible thing in the room.

Eventually Lambert said, 'Where were you last night, Mr Warner?'

Warner ran his hands swiftly through his fair hair; his blue eyes were wide with an entreaty that he should be believed. He said without looking at his wife beside him, 'We were here, both of us. You tend to be, when you have young children.'

Hook, looking up calmly from his recording of their replies said, 'Is there anyone outside the family who could confirm that for us?'

Joyce Warner said, 'I had a phone call from a friend, but it was quite late; after ten, I suppose. The only other thing is a kind of negative evidence: we can't go out without a babysitter, and you won't find anyone who sat for us last night.'

She sounded very calm, as if she had been expecting this: perhaps their earlier questions about the whereabouts of her brother had alerted her to the possibility. They were vouching for each other, of course, as husband and wife often did. But they were not stupid; they must know that either one of them could have been out for most of the evening.

At length, Mark Warner said in a dry voice, 'Surely the probable explanation is that this gardener boy—Everton Smith, is it?—killed Laura and hanged himself in remorse, realizing that it was only a matter of time before you came to arrest him.'

Lambert allowed himself a small, mirthless smile. 'I said Mr Smith was found hanging. I didn't say he hanged himself. I'm now quite certain, in fact, that he didn't. He was killed quite deliberately, by the same person who murdered Mrs Pritchard.'

It was the first time Lambert had put it into words. Bert Hook felt that he had known it from the moment when he had heard of Smith's death.

## CHAPTER EIGHTEEN

It was the barman at the golf club who told Jim Pritchard about this new death.

'Remember that black lad we had working on the course last year? Nice lad: always cheerful, he was. Good-looking, I suppose, in his own way.' After this startling exhibition of enlightened liberalism, he carried on polishing a glass, his hands working automatically, his eyes on the face of the Chairman of the Greens Committee.

'Remember him? I employ him, George! He does gardening at my house. Poor Laura had become quite attached to him.'

A CID man would have noted his use of the present tense about the dead man; the distinction was rather wasted on George, who was full of his news. He said, with that mixture of awe and relish which the man in the street brings to melodrama, 'Well, you won't be employing him any more, I'm afraid. He's dead, you see. Topped himself, last night.'

'Good heavens! I was talking to him at the house only a couple of days ago. He should have been coming again on Friday.'

George had had half an hour on his own before the bar opened to assimilate the death and ruminate about its implications. He said, 'Do you think it means that young Everton—' and then stopped. He must not put his conjectures to Mr Pritchard, who was too immediately involved in this with the death of his wife. Bad taste, that would be.

Jim Pritchard did not seem to be upset by the barman's gaffe. He said, 'Where was this? At that place where he lived?' He made it sound as though suicide was only to be expected in such a setting, the kind of thing which happened daily in Jackson Terrace.

'No, it was miles from there; somewhere near the Severn, I think. He topped himself in an empty cottage, I believe.' The truth had not yet been much distorted: as it passed through different mouths, it would become ever less accurate and more lurid.

Jim Pritchard had not been playing golf, so that there had been no need to shower or change before he went into the bar. He was the first person in there when it opened; he was glad of that, for it meant that he had no need to listen to other reactions to the barman's sensational revelations. He drank the single pint he had permitted himself on this warm morning, replying conventionally to George's more careful speculations, leaving as soon as other members began to filter into the bar after their morning rounds.

He drove out past the eighth hole, where an hour previously he had been inspecting the clearance of the tangle of scrub and saplings from behind the green. He waved to the course staff, now walking towards the green-keepers' shed for their lunch break. Then he pressed the button and lowered the front windows of the Jaguar fully, savouring the smell of the warm, damp earth. He had enjoyed determining the positions of the pot-grown rhododendrons they were going to put in here. He could not admit it, of course, even to himself, but he sometimes relished walking round the course with his proprietorial air, making small decisions at the tactful prompting of the head green-keeper, more than he enjoyed his golf. Well, everyone knew what a frustrating game it could be when the ball refused to go into the hole.

And he was quite ready to find the police car at his door. George's news had prepared him for that. But he had rather expected Lambert and that burly sergeant who seemed to act as his amanuensis. He had not met the dark-haired, earnest young man who walked ramrod-straight over the gravel to meet him. 'Detective Inspector Christopher Rushton,' the man said, his delivery as stiff as his walk, offering the owner of this impressive house his full name, as if he was determined to assert his right to be here as formally as possible.

They went inside to the privacy of the study. Jim realized that the young man—anyone around thirty was definitely young nowadays—was studying his behaviour closely. No doubt he had learned to treat grieving widowers with kid gloves, but it was a little disconcerting. Rushton appeared to be in no hurry: he waited until they were both seated before he said, 'There have been further developments, Mr Pritchard.'

Jim said, 'I know. I heard at the golf club. I'm told that my gardener, Everton Smith, has hanged himself.'

Irritation came and went as swiftly as a nervous tic from Rushton's face. Such things should not get abroad until they were officially released, but he was getting used to living in an imperfect world. He ran his fingers lightly over the cuff of his immaculate dark suit and searched the tanned face opposite him for any information it might unwittingly offer. 'When did you last see Mr Smith?'

It was the first time Jim had ever heard the title afforded to the lithe young man who had tended the lawns outside his window. Perhaps death warranted a little dignity, however superficial. 'Everton was last here on Monday. Your Superintendent Lambert and his sergeant came here to see him then.'

'And you have not see him since that day?'

'No. I've just said that.'

'To be precise, you told me when he was last here, sir. Have you any knowledge of his movements in the last two days?'

Jim Pritchard told himself that he must not allow himself to lose patience with this jumped-up young man. Even that phrase was a warning as it came leaping into his mind; he must be more neutral, more careful of his attitudes. He did not wish to lose control of this exchange, whatever the temptations he was offered to do so. 'Of course I don't know where Smith has been in the last two days. He was a jobbing gardener here, no more.'

'Mr Lambert saw him at the beginning of his work period here, I believe. No doubt you spoke to him later in the day?'

'I talked to him briefly when I paid him, yes. He didn't tell me he was planning to top himself, if that's what you're thinking.' Jim's white teeth flashed into a sneer beneath the two inches of black moustache. It was not very effective contempt, because scorn needs some sort of reaction if it is not to fall flat. He was sorry immediately that he had been drawn into the barman's phrase: it made him sound uncaring. He sought out the obvious excuse. 'Look, you can hardly expect me to be heartbroken to find that the young lout who killed my wife has decided to end his problems. If you ask me, we're all well rid of him. Saves the expense of a trial, for a start.'

'Oh, I think there'll be a trial, Mr Pritchard. But not of Everton Smith, naturally. Did he give you any impression that he might be frightened? Any sense that he felt that his life might be in danger?'

'No . . . No, he didn't. Look, are you saying that young Smith—'

'Do you know of anyone who might have wished to harm Mr Smith?'

'No.' Jim made a determined effort to reform his tone to one of concern. He could hear the gears changing himself as he said, 'I didn't know anything about his life away from here, Inspector. I don't suppose I spoke to him more than two or three times throughout his time here. Laura could no doubt have told you a lot more than I can.'

'So you will have no idea how he acquired a large sum of money at around the time of your wife's death?' Rushton made ignorance sound like a major sin of omission.

'No.'

'Where were you last night, Mr Pritchard?'

Pritchard stroked his moustache, his mind working furiously. 'I live alone here now. You wouldn't expect me to have witnesses to my every movement. Fortunately, I was at the golf club for most of the evening.'

'Until when?'

'Until about nine, I suppose. The steward will confirm it for you.'

'I've no doubt he will, sir, in due course. Where did you go when you left the golf club?'

'I came back here.'

'And you were here for the rest of the night?'

'Yes. And there are no witnesses to that. But you wouldn't expect there to be.'

Rushton noted the replies diligently and went away to feed them into his computer record. He wondered how many of the suspects would have a better alibi for last night than Jim Pritchard, who stood at the window of his study until the police car moved out of his sight. The Warners were alibi-ing each other, which to a suspicious policeman meant they had no alibis at all. He wondered what the enigmatic Sue Hendry and that strange man Peter Brooke would have to offer. For what it was worth, his money for this one would be on the man he had just left, but he had been wrong too often in the past to risk voicing that to his colleagues.

There was an instruction for him from John Lambert when he got back to the Murder Room. He picked up the phone and got in touch with the Firearm Licences Department to implement it immediately. Then he wondered why Lambert was suddenly checking on the possession of firearms among their five remaining suspects.

Gloucester has nothing like the social disturbance or the violence of London. But it has its fair share of these things, like any British city of any size in the 'nineties.

Amongst the other flotsam of the enterprise society, it has its homeless and its buskers. The latter operate mostly in the pedestrian precinct around the major shops of the city centre—there are few subways to offer shelter and funnel the crowds past them in this ancient town. The police do not as yet consider the buskers a major problem: there are not very many of them, and they do not appear to have close connections with that sub-culture of drugs and petty crime which is making the centres of some major British cities places of fear and squalor.

Once the CID thought of extending their search to Gloucester, it did not take the uniformed men long to bring in Peter Brooke. He was too good a violinist to remain anonymous among the motley collection of folk-singers and guitar players who predominated in this bohemian company. He had even managed to attract a small audience who paused to listen, rather than dropping their charity into the hat as they hurried on in embarrassment. Not many buskers chose Sarasate, and none of them played it with that mixture of fine tone and spirited attack.

He was uneasy at the police station, unable to keep

his limbs still, spilling the mug of tea he was eventually given on the front of his already stained and torn sweater, then cupping his hands round it like an old man to retain control of it. It seemed amazing that he should have such immediate control of the violin whenever his hands fell into position upon it, but policemen are used to such contradictions.

When they put him into the interview room, his dark, deep-set eyes looked around with the quick, desperate glances of a caged animal. He was persuaded to sit down, but when Bert Hook came with a young detective constable to interview him, he was standing again in the corner of the tiny room, stooping like one carrying many more than his twenty-eight years.

He had not shaved for two days at least. By his appearance and his odour, he had not washed either. There was a stale smell about him, a compound of bad breath, stale food, and dirty clothes. In the confines of the green-walled interview room, there was no escaping from it. Bert had smelt worse: at least there was no vomit to contend with here. He began with the routine admonishment. 'You were asked to keep us informed of your whereabouts. You didn't do that.'

Brooke looked as if he didn't even understand. He scratched his cheek for a couple of seconds before he said, 'I'm "of no fixed abode". That's what the pig wrote in the book in London.'

'But we know where your squat is, and you weren't there.'

'I was there until . . .'—he paused and looked thoroughly confused—'until two or three days ago.'

Hook wondered if he knew what day it was as they spoke. He said, 'And where have you been for those two or three days?'

The dark eyes peered at him suspiciously from beneath their unkempt brows, searching for the trap which lay behind the words. 'In Gloucester. I wasn't trying to hide.'

Hook smiled. 'If you had been, playing your fiddle in front of the Guildhall wouldn't have been the best way to do it. Especially as they tell me you play it rather well. But you didn't sleep in Eastgate Street. Where have you spent the nights, Mr Brooke?'

Again Brooke paused, as though trying to work out what net was being spread for him beneath the unfamiliar 'Mr' and the compliment to his musicianship. 'Near the docks. Behind Baxter's warehouse. I grew up round here, you know: I know my way round.'

There was a small, bitter pride in his voice. In London, he had needed to be shown the ropes by other, more experienced members of the human detritus who slept rough each night in that metropolis of modern civilization. Coming back to his roots, he had been able to fend for himself without such guidance, even in his present wretched state.

Hook looked at the thin arms, clasped around the violin case as though it was a baby that someone might try to take away at any moment. 'It's still cold at nights. Near freezing, wasn't it, last night?'

'We have boxes. Big, cardboard boxes; there are plenty of them round there.' Despite his initial, automatic use of 'pig', he was being won round—too easily, some of his streetwise London companions would have said. He had delivered his latest reply in an educated voice, speaking standard English, with only the faintest trace of a local accent. It came oddly from this stinking, scarecrow figure.

'Do you take drugs, Mr Brooke?'

He was neither surprised nor shocked by the question. For the first time, he did not hesitate over his reply, and for the first time it was clear and precise. 'No. I have done in the past, but only pot. I've never touched coke or heroin.' He looked suddenly younger, like an earnest adolescent trying to convince them. Bert Hook caught a glimpse of the boy who had gone off happily to the Royal College of Music with the world at his feet. Brooke said, 'I'm not a pusher, if that's what you think.'

'No, I don't think that, Peter. But I thought you might be a user. You must admit that you've been behaving strangely in the last month. I don't know how things were before that.'

Brooke looked as if he was considering this view of himself for the first time. Then he nodded, as if it had surprised him. 'I suppose I have.'

Hook looked at the dirt beneath the fingernails that were so prominent on top of the violin case. 'Can you give us any explanation for your behaviour? It's time you did.'

Most young men would have thought the grief following inevitably on the murder of a mother, even when she was estranged from her son, was sufficient explanation for some erratic conduct. Brooke did not even proffer it as the cause, except indirectly. 'I thought you'd have me in the frame for my mother's murder, once you knew how I'd hated her. And I told you that myself.'

'I can understand how you thought that. But it wasn't the best policy to lie to us. Once we find one lie, we wonder how many more you've tried to sell to us. In your case, we're still wondering.'

Brooke nodded; an intelligent young man giving his attention to a serious suggestion, his attitude again at odds with his vagrant's appearance. Hook reminded himself that these sudden switches of attention and mood could be symptomatic of irresponsible, murderous minds; sometimes they went with that absence of any moral awareness that characterizes the psychopath. Bert said, with the air of an older man giving good advice, 'You should tell me now when you last saw your mother, and what went on between the two of you in those last meetings.'

The man with the violin nodded seriously, for all the world as if he were accepting a precept from Menuhin in a master class, as he once had in happier days. He seemed now to have lost all fear of his interviewer. After a moment of intense thought, he said, 'It was on the Friday before she died.'

It was impossible to be sure whether Hook was encouraging or gently threatening as he said, 'There are witnesses to that meeting. You had better tell us what happened.'

This time there was no hesitation. It was clear that Brooke had been over this many times in his own mind: it was only naming the exact day which had caused him to pause over his reply. 'I went to The Beeches to see Laura. My sister Joyce had persuaded me to do that. She said that Mother wanted to be reconciled and that I should give her a chance.'

Not that they should make up their differences, or any such phrase, thought Bert. The young usually saw things not only in black and white but entirely from their own point of view. From what he had heard, Laura Pritchard had in this case been much at fault, but doubtless not exclusively. The dead are never able to put forward their case for consideration. He thought for a moment of the source of their information about this Friday meeting, Sue Hendry, with her very different perception of the dead woman. 'And did you see in fact see her as you had planned?'

'Yes. Joyce dropped me off in the village and I walked up to the house. I didn't want to present myself under big sister's wing, you see. Some woman drove up to The Beeches and dropped Laura off from a car. She passed me in the lane on her way back, but I didn't recognize her.'

'Sue Hendry. She manages your mother's secretarial agency.'

And she was also her lover, expecting to set up house with her. No need to tell him that.

He nodded, seemingly anxious only to recall the detail and tell his tale. 'I went into the house and spoke with

Laura. Jim Pritchard wasn't there. Laura said he'd gone into Cheltenham to get some gear for his holiday.'

'What was it you wanted to see her about?'

'I'd decided to go back to college. My sister had been trying to persuade me to complete the course for years. I needed money to do it—I'd forfeited any right to a grant by throwing up the course in mid-year when Dad died. I'd sworn I'd never speak to Laura again when Mandy died in India—you know about her?'

Hook nodded. 'Your sister told us.'

He looked relieved not to have to relive that episode. 'Well, Laura said she was ready to help. Eager to, in fact. Joyce had said she would be, if only I would take the first step and make contact.'

'How long were you there?'

Again that serious look came over the filthy face. His forehead creased itself into a little frown of concentration which was oddly reminiscent of his sister. 'Not long. I suppose about twenty minutes. It was the first amicable exchange we'd had in several years, and I think neither of us wanted to push it too far. There was too much between us for it to be called a reconciliation. It might have been the beginning of one.' He was picking his words precisely, weighing them like a university don. The contrast between his speech and his appearance would have been comic, had this not been such a serious business for the men on both sides of the small square table with its silently turning cassette recorder.

'And you left the way you had come?'

'Yes. Laura couldn't give me a lift back to the village because her husband had her car—I think she said his was being serviced. And I didn't want to meet the man who had taken my father's place.' His face darkened at the thought. He sounded almost like Hamlet, whom Bert had studied on his Open University foundation course; but there was no sign of an Oedipus complex here.

'Did anyone see you go?'

'No. Not that I know of. Why?'

'Because it would be nice to have some confirmation, first that you left when you say you did and secondly that the meeting was as amicable as you contend it was.'

'Jim Pritchard must have come home not very long after I left.'

'But he hasn't told us that his wife even mentioned that you had been.'

He gave serious thought to the matter in his curious, academic way, with his chin lifted and his eyes cast above their heads; he looked as though he was deliberating some minor point of literary criticism with a college tutor, rather than trying to convince policemen of his innocence of murder. 'No, it's quite possible that she wouldn't have told him. She knew I didn't want my business discussed with him. And I got the impression that things weren't too close between them, from the way she spoke of him.'

That showed some perception, if what he was saying was true. He could not have known that she was planning to leave her husband to set up house with Sue Hendry. But that in turn assumed that the doughty Miss Hendry was telling them the truth about the affair, and also that Laura Pritchard had not been deceiving her. There were far too many ifs and buts in this case. Hook dropped his next question in without the hint of a change in tone: even the young DC at his side only realized how important it was when he saw the reaction of the man who sat opposite. 'And why did you go back to The Beeches to see your mother again on the following Monday, Peter?'

Brooke looked first surprised and then apprehensive, as if the trust which this ruddy-cheeked countryman had won from him had been used to set a trap for him. 'I—I didn't go there on the Monday.'

Hook raised his eyebrows, looked in puzzlement at the officer beside him, riffled for the first time through the papers he had brought with him. It took several seconds, and it was a convincing performance. 'Our information is that you were.'

'Then your information is wrong. The last time I saw my mother was on that Friday afternoon.' He hugged his violin case hard, swaying gently backwards and forwards on the unyielding upright chair. His dark eyes never left Hook's, but there was fear in them now, as well as a desire to convince.

Hook looked regretful, studied his papers again for a moment, said quietly, 'Do you know a chap called Everton Smith? He did gardening for your mother at The Beeches. She used to work with him in the gardens.'

'I don't know the name. Is he a coloured boy? Quite young; cheerful-looking; with a Honda 750?'

'That's the chap. I didn't think you'd be into motor-bikes.'

'Oh, I used to be, when Dad was alive. Had a little Honda myself once, before I went to college. Never got to the big stuff.' He looked delighted to have surprised them with this. Perhaps no one had taken much interest in what he thought and knew for a long time, so that even this sort of interest pleased him. They were getting a glimpse of the naturally gregarious boy he must have been before life went seriously wrong for him.

'The gardener's name was Everton Smith. It was he who said he'd seen you on the Monday.'

'No, he's got it wrong. He did see me on the Friday, though; he's probably just made a mistake about the day. Don't forget it's almost three weeks ago now. I should ask him again.' Perhaps he became aware of how closely they were studying him throughout this. Certainly he now checked himself and said apprehensively, 'What's wrong? He hasn't told you anything else, has he?'

Hook waited, but Brooke said nothing to incriminate himself. For ten seconds, he studied the grubby countenance opposite him as carefully as if it had been a slide under a microscope. Finally he asked, 'Where were you last night, Peter?'

The deep-set eyes widened in alarm. 'I told you: behind Baxter's warehouse. Why?'

'Before that. Where were you during the evening?'

'I played some Bach in the pedestrian precinct for a while. There weren't a lot of people about, but I like playing Bach, anyway. Until about eight, I suppose—I don't have a watch. After that . . .' His forehead puckered again in that frown that was so like his sister's. Then his face brightened. 'We had fish and chips. I'd done quite well with the busking, and I treated a lad who plays the flute—he's quite good, but it's not a popular instrument for busking, the flute. Not solo, anyway.' For a moment, he was diverted into the intricacies of the public taste in its entertainers.

Hook said, 'Can you find him for us? You may have to.'

Brooke was brought back to the thought of murder as much by the sober tone of this as the content. 'I think so. I don't know Tony's second name, but he's probably still working the patch near the Guildhall.'

'And was he with you throughout the night?'

'No. He sleeps at home. He just can't get a job in music. Not for the moment.' He made it sound as if his new friend's integrity was more important than the proof of his own whereabouts.

'Is there anyone, then, who can vouch for your being in Gloucester between nine o'clock and midnight last night?'

He thought, brought back again to his own danger. 'No, I don't think so. Not for the whole of that time. I dossed down early—you get the most sheltered places, in the doorways and entrances, if you're down before the pubs empty. There were others there when I got up this morning, but I don't know when they arrived.'

'Do you drive?'

'I can do, yes. I passed when I was eighteen. And I have

a full motorcycle licence. Why is it important? Tell me what happened last night!' His voice had for the first time a hint of hysteria.

Hood studied him for a moment before he said, 'Everton Smith, who claimed to have seen you at The Beeches on that Monday, was murdered last night, Peter. Almost certainly by the same hand that killed your mother.'

In the moment in which Brooke looked at them, his features filled with dread as he appreciated the purpose of their previous questions. Then he plunged his face abruptly into his hands.

The policemen, professionally objective, watched the filthy fingers trying to restrain the tearless sobs of the face behind them; beneath them, the arms were still clasped awkwardly around the battered violin case.

## CHAPTER NINETEEN

While Lambert chafed through the morning in a regional CID meeting, the case ground inexorably forward.

The preliminary report from forensic confirmed that Everton Smith had died by hanging. There was one interesting and puzzling subsidiary fact: the laboratory tests had revealed no sign of scuffing from the corpse's heavy boots on the wood taken to the laboratory for examination.

Hook had his pie and pint in the snug of the White Lion hotel which was adjacent to the Oldford CID section. The fare was no better than average, but the room had a television set, and he timed his visit carefully to get half an hour of the test match. The England seamers were being put to the sword and the pub's armchair experts were suitably scathing in their assessments. Bert, who had rarely overrated the opposition in his own playing days, thought privately that the Australian strokeplay was rather impressive.

When he returned to the station, he rang Brooke Office Services and tried to make an appointment to see Sue Hendry with Lambert during the afternoon, but the receptionist was at first evasive and then defensive of her employer. Hook was polite but determined: he had pinned down reluctant citizens too often to be easily turned aside. Eventually the woman allowed a little of her irritation to slip through her loyalty.

'Miss Hendry rang in only a few minutes ago. Said she couldn't quite say when she would be in. It's very inconvenient, especially now that Mrs Pritchard isn't around to help out. She has some important appointments this afternoon. I'll just have to try to see them myself, but they won't be very pleased to be dealt with by an underling.'

'Men, are they?'

She giggled briefly. 'Yes, they are mostly. Rather pompous men, actually, two of them.'

'I'm sure you'll be more than a match for them. Behave like the newest director of the firm, not an underling.'

'H'm. I'm paid as an underling . . . Actually, I'm a bit worried about Sue—Miss Hendry.'

'Did she seem upset?'

'Yes, I suppose she did, a little.' She spoke reluctantly, as if to reveal so much was in some way unfair to a woman for whom she felt both friendship and a great professional respect.

'Distraught, even?' Hook prompted quietly.

There was a silence while the receptionist assessed the word. 'Ye-es, I suppose so . . . You don't think there's anything wrong, do you?'

'I shouldn't think so. But we'll probably check, just to be certain. So don't worry about her.'

'I only noticed she was upset because it's so unusual. There's no one calmer as a rule, you see. She never brings her home problems to work.' It was a belated attempt to defend her sex against the tiresome male charge of emotionalism.

Hook rang off quickly. Then he tried Sue Hendry's home number immediately. He let the phone ring on for a long time when she did not answer. The regular tones seemed suddenly ominous, as though they were informing him and only him that the woman was in some kind of danger. He was glad to hear Lambert's voice speaking to Rushton in the corridor outside. It was not only receptionists, he reflected, who sought the comfort of a higher rank to take responsibility.

Lambert moved with relief from a morning spent discussing the generalities of police crime-solving strategy to the sharp focus of a particular criminal investigation. He listened with only two sharp questions to Rushton's account of his meeting with Jim Pritchard, then asked the DI to stay with him whilst Hook came in to discuss his interview of Peter Brooke.

After many years of practice, Hook was an expert in assessing his chief's mood. He took one look at him and delivered his facts briskly, with a minimum of speculation. But at the end he did say, 'Brooke had the opportunity for both murders, though he denies being at The Beeches on the Monday when Smith said he saw him there.'

Rushton said, 'And do you see him as a killer?'

A little flick of irritation passed across Hook's rounded features. He suspected—quite wrongly in this case—that Rushton was trying to probe his reputed preference for the underdog. There was an old barrier between the two of them, erected at the time when Bert had years ago turned down the promotion to Inspector which Rushton had chased so eagerly. Integrity, whatever its roots, has a habit of making colleagues uneasy.

Bert said stiffly, 'I have an open mind about Brooke. He has clearly been very disturbed, though he seems to me to be coming out of the phase. But I don't think he has been going through the kind of emotional upset that finds its outlet in violence. And I don't think he's a natural liar. But we need to stick to the facts; and the facts say that Brooke's a suspect.'

It was always a safe ploy to stress the importance of facts with Lambert, who could be a positive Gradgrind when it came to establishing the framework of a case. It was Lambert who now grunted, 'We only have Smith's word for it that Brooke was at The Beeches on that Monday, of course. No one else has reported seeing Brooke, though a couple of people in the village think they recall seeing Smith's motorbike on that day.'

Lambert pushed himself back in his chair and shut his eyes. For five seconds, his ageing face was as still and unrevealing as a lizard's. Then he sought out another fact. Opening his grey eyes and switching them swiftly to Rushton, he asked, 'Did you get that information from the Firearms Licences section, Chris?'

Rushton could not suppress a small smile of satisfaction at his own efficiency. 'There is only one firearm recorded among our chief suspects. A Smith and Wesson .38 pistol. Not new, but quite adequate to kill a man. There may of course be shotguns among the others without any record, especially if they've been held for a few years.'

Hook said, 'What is the significance of a firearm, when both of our victims were garrotted?'

Lambert grinned; it lasted no more than a second, but perhaps he had been hoping for the query. 'There may be none at all, Bert. But if I'm right about the manner of Everton Smith's dying, someone must have forced him to put that rope around his neck: it's not a thing you could kid a man into doing. The easiest form of threat is a firearm, where one is readily available.' He turned back to Rushton. 'Which of our suspects is the proud and legal possessor of a Smith and Wesson, Chris?'

The DI smiled grimly. It seemed that for once his own

choice of killer might be justified. He said quietly, 'It's registered in the name of James Pritchard.'

Lambert drove with uncharacteristic urgency on this last journey to The Beeches. Twice the wheels of the old Vauxhall squealed in protest as he threw it round tight bends in the lanes.

They were almost halfway to the house when Bert Hook, catching his breath at this frantic new rhythm, thought to mention that he had not succeeded in arranging the planned interview with Sue Hendry.

Lambert's eyes narrowed, but did not stray from the tarmac which was flying beneath his wheels. 'Where is she, Bert?'

'The girl at the office didn't know. She was a bit put out about it, actually. Miss Hendry apparently had some important clients booked in for this afternoon. But she rang through about half an hour ago to say she wouldn't be coming in.'

'Why?'

'The girl couldn't say. She thought her boss sounded rather upset. I tried to get her myself, but there was no reply.'

'Try her now on that thing.' Lambert gestured towards the car phone for which he always professed such distaste. Hook, averting his eyes resolutely from the flying hedgerows, concentrated on tapping out Sue Hendry's home number. There was again no reply.

If anything, Lambert seemed to drive even more quickly. Hook was relieved when they screeched to a stop amid flying gravel at the door of The Beeches. That gravel and the manner of their arrival meant that there was no chance of taking Pritchard by surprise. But greater stealth would not have produced a different result. The house was empty.

Hook was out of the car as it lurched to a halt, hurrying away to the garage as bidden in search of the evidence which might imprison a murderer for life. Lambert made a swift tour of the outside of the house, satisfying himself that neither Pritchard nor anyone else was within it. He had the Vauxhall turned and revving beside the garage when Hook emerged from it, panting but grimly successful.

The shortest route to Sue Hendry's home, using the intricate network of minor roads which were the product of an earlier agrarian age, was no longer than eight miles. With Hook holding the map book in trembling fingers and issuing directions more calmly than he would have believed possible, they covered the distance in eleven minutes.

Miss Hendry's home would have brought forth the automatic adjective of 'charming' from any estate agent. It was in fact one of a pair of cottages fashioned from the conversion of a small stable block. The Victorian house which had once been the centre of the little complex had long disappeared, and there appeared to be no one at home in the other cottage which adjoined that of the manager of Brooke Office Services.

There was only one vehicle in sight as the old Vauxhall halted abruptly at the entrance. But it was one which sent Lambert through the low wooden gate and up the garden at a run. For it was Jim Pritchard's blue Jaguar.

The porch door was open. The inner door was shut but not locked. Lambert and Hook passed in quick succession into the house; neither of them even considered ringing the bell which was clearly visible amongst the clematis which clambered over the porch in innocent profusion.

After the June day outside, the room they entered was suddenly dark. The lightest things in it were the two white faces which swung towards them with their entry. Jim Pritchard stood at one side of the empty fireplace, his elbow upon the mantelpiece. It was a casual pose, but the tension of his body seemed to deny its informality; it looked as though it had been hastily assumed with the noise of their entry into the house.

On the other side of the fireplace, Sue Hendry sat with her hands grasping the wooden arms of her fireside chair. Her face was the colour of ivory, but relief rushed into it even as the two policemen stopped, breathing heavily in the silent room.

It was Jim Pritchard who was the first to move. He took a pace away from the fireplace and seated himself in the corresponding armchair to the one occupied by the woman whose eyes stared unblinkingly at his face. He leaned back determinedly, clasping his arms over the ends of the chair's arms, but again gave the impression of a man simulating relaxation rather than a genuinely relaxed one.

But his self-discipline was impressive. He looked up at Lambert, who now towered above him as he held himself steady in the high-backed armchair, and measured his words as he said, 'I'm glad you've arrived, Superintendent. Miss Hendry has become a little hysterical, I'm afraid. She's made accusations which I'm sure would bring me handsome libel payments if she chose to repeat them in public. I accept that she was a close friend of my wife's, and thus has some excuse to be overwrought.' He switched his attention from Lambert to the widening eyes of the woman who sat opposite him. 'But you really must learn to keep a rein on that tongue of yours, my dear.'

The last phrase was even more of a mistake than the smile with which he accompanied it. It transformed the fear which had held Sue Hendry rigid into anger. And with rage came a new animation, as if someone had set a torch to dry timber. Colour sprang back into her face: in seconds her cheeks were almost as bright as the red hair above them. Beneath the sandy eyebrows, her green eyes flashed with a wild challenge; her whole body trembled with passion as she shifted to the very edge of her seat. For a moment, Hook thought she was going to spring across the room at Pritchard; he took two swift paces to her side, ready to restrain her if necessary.

She reminded Lambert no longer of the sturdy hockey player but of a wounded tiger. But she made no move towards her prey. Whilst she addressed her words to Lambert in a surprisingly even tone, she kept her gaze unblinkingly upon the face of Pritchard. 'He killed Laura, Superintendent. I don't know all the details yet, but he killed my Laura.'

'*Your* Laura? She wasn't *your* Laura, you perverted little cow!' The equanimity which Pritchard had so carefully assumed was shattered in a flash with her assertion of possession. He glanced up at the man whose restraining hand was now upon his shoulder and attempted too late to regain his composure. 'Laura was my wife. If you had the slightest sensitivity you'd curb your wild accusations at a time like this.'

'You killed her, and we both know it.'

Pritchard forced himself to smile at her. 'May I remind you that I was not even in the country when Laura was killed. Superintendent Lambert at least knows that, even if you aren't able to see things straight.' He looked up at Lambert, spreading his hands wide in a gesture that was meant to say, 'Lord preserve all of us from emotional females!' It had the air of a bad stage gesture, for his limbs were too stiff to allow him the relaxation the thought needed.

Sue Hendry was not diverted. The arrival of the two policemen had released her from all fear. Her gaze still fixed upon Pritchard's face, which seemed in this subdued light to have lost all its holiday tan, she said through lips which scarcely opened, 'I haven't worked out how he did it yet, but I know he did. Perhaps you hired someone to kill her whilst you were safely out of the way.'

Pritchard tried righteous indignation. 'I've really had quite enough of these preposterous suggestions. I've tried to be patient because you were a trusted employee of my wife. Now I realize that it was useless to come here and try to calm you down. I think it is time I went.'

'You came here to threaten me! To shut me up.' A new horror flashed into her revealing features. 'I expect you killed the gardening boy as well. And you came here today to shut me up—' Her fist, clenched tight with the full impact of his wickedness and her danger, flashed up against her mouth; her knuckles were almost as white as the teeth which closed upon them to prevent any sound issuing.

Lambert decided he had waited long enough for his man to make false moves. He said calmly, 'I don't think he employed anyone else to kill his wife, Miss Hendry. I'm quite sure he killed her himself.'

Probably Pritchard knew at that moment that it was over. If so, he gave little sign of it. Perhaps he whitened a little beneath that fading tan; perhaps there was just too long a pause before he gathered himself to say, 'Now I *am* going to get annoyed, Superintendent. This woman has some excuse for her wild accusations, but you on the other hand—'

Lambert cut through his words, continuing to speak over the head of the sitting man to the woman opposite him. 'He killed her, you see, before he left. Garrotted her with a cord, took her body to the Severn in her own car, tied weights to her ankles, and dumped her in the river.' He was at his most ruthless now; in his anxiety to provoke an indiscretion from the man to complete his case, he did not spare the feelings of the woman as he saw her gasping with shock at the details.

For the first time since they had arrived, Pritchard's voice lurched as he delivered the stage villain's desperate line, 'You'd better have some proof for this!'

There was the slightest nod from Lambert to Hook, which all but the keenest observer would have missed. The sergeant took a quick look at Sue Hendry, decided she was no longer in danger of springing upon her adversary, and moved upon silent feet into the hall. A moment later, he reappeared with the thing he had left there as he and Lambert made their precipitate entry into the cottage. He stood there a little self-consciously as all the eyes in the room turned upon him.

Had the stakes not been so high, it might have been a moment of bathos. He held aloft nothing more sinister than a sturdy blue wooden stool. He clutched it gingerly by one of its feet, round which he had wrapped a piece of polythene, in preparation for the time when it was produced for the jury's inspection as an exhibit in a murder trial. Standing in the doorway with the stool held in front of him, he looked, as Pritchard half-rose at the sight, incongruously like a lion-tamer.

The effect upon Pritchard was visible. As he sank back into the armchair, he said, 'What on earth are you doing with that? And who the hell gave you permission to lay your hands upon my property?' But it was no more than bluster, and all four people in the room suddenly knew it.

Lambert placed his hand firmly on the shoulder beneath him and said, 'James Pritchard, I am arresting you for the murders of Laura Jane Pritchard and Everton Smith. You are not obliged to say anything. Anything you do say may be used in evidence.'

The ritual words of the arrest rang like a knell in the sudden heavy silence. Pritchard looked from one to the other of the two CID men, who were watchful now against any attempt at escape. He did not even glance at the woman he had come here to silence. For a moment the harshness of his breathing was magnified by the silence of the others in that low-ceilinged cottage room. Then his shoulders dropped and he said simply, 'How did you know?'

It was the sort of phrase Lambert was anxious to hear. It seemed that he had got his caution in just in time. As Hook went into the hall to radio for a squad car to come out and pick up their man, his chief said quietly, 'I didn't know for certain until you killed young Smith. Violence breeds more violence, as people like us have come to know better than most. You should never have gone on to a second murder.'

'I had no choice. He was scared. He was going to tell you. I had to get rid of him.' One by one, the staccato sentences dropped horribly into the room. This was the pragmatism of evil, with all morality thrust aside.

Lambert fed him the questions, giving him the rope to hang himself, wishing at that moment that that could be more than a metaphor. 'Did he know that you were going to kill your wife?'

Pritchard stroked his moustache, a gesture with which he unconsciously accompanied cogitation. He appeared to be considering the matter for the first time. 'No, I don't suppose he did. He should have done, but he wasn't too bright. If he had been, he'd have made sure you didn't find out about the money as easily as you did.'

'You paid him to say your wife was still alive on the Monday after you'd gone to Spain.'

'Yes. He'd have had the second half of the payment when everything was safely over, but he was running scared. Said he didn't realize that there was any plan to kill Laura when he agreed to take the money. Did he think I'd pay that sort of sum to scum like him if I wasn't up to something serious? He had to go.' He nodded his head sharply several times, as if confirming the perfect logic of his actions to himself. Then, for all the world as if he was discussing the key to an innocent puzzle, he said, 'What made you think it was me in the first place?'

'A number of things. Your alibi was laid on a little too thickly. Leaving the service bill with the car mileage on the front seat of your Jaguar showed that it had not been used to transport the body. But it was so convenient and obvious that it looked a little suspicious. And once forensic showed us that your wife's car had been used to transport the corpse, you were always the likeliest person to have used it—once we could prove that you were around at the time when the murder was committed. You were driving your wife's car on the Friday before you went away: no doubt you killed her that night.'

'Yes. And disposed of her. The bitch!' His hatred rang out for the first time. It was a relief to him to abandon dissimulation. Bert Hook put a restraining hand on Sue Hendry, but she made no move towards the man who had killed the person she had loved.

Lambert, playing his fish carefully, let a moment elapse before he said simply, 'Why, Mr Pritchard?'

The man in the armchair looked up at him blankly. It seemed he could not believe anyone would need telling what was so clearly self-evident. 'Because she was about to go off with this little red-haired cow, of course! Going to bed with her. Setting up house with her.'

'And you thought that enough reason for murder?'

'She was going to announce that she preferred a woman to me. She was out to make me a laughing stock!'

For a man of Pritchard's temperament and social milieu, that was probably the most important consideration of all. Lambert could imagine the sensational whispers running round that bastion of traditional prejudices, Pritchard's golf club. He fed him another suggestion. 'So you planned to make it look as if you were out of the country when it happened.'

Pritchard nodded, almost smiled. 'She'd already written the notes for the milkman and the cleaner. I gave them to Smith and arranged for him to put them out when he came on the Monday. The milkman left double milk for the weekend on the Saturday. All Smith had to do was to pour it away, wash the bottles, and put them out with the note early on Monday morning.'

'And to say that he'd seen Peter Brooke here then?'

'No. He put that in off his own bat. I know he saw him here on the Friday, so I expect he thought he'd include that as part of his day's gardening on the Monday.' He shook his head over such initiative, for all the world like a man lamenting the quality of modern domestic staff. He looked up at Lambert. 'Why didn't you believe that Laura was still alive on the Monday, as Smith told you?'

'Police procedures have their uses. The house-to-house inquiries turned up no one else in the village who had seen your wife after Friday. And although you didn't know it, Laura had arranged to meet Miss Hendry here once you had gone on Saturday. If Laura had been alive, she would almost surely have let her know about any change of plan.'

Pritchard, who had been treating a murder investigation as if it had been no more than the story of a missed train, now flashed a look of molten hatred at the woman on the other side of the fireplace. It was returned with interest. It was Pritchard who eventually dropped his eyes; he said in a flat, defeated voice, 'I should never have used that black bastard. He wasn't up to it.'

'Fortunately, not many people are up to murder. How did you get him out to the barn to kill him?'

Pritchard made no attempt now to deny this second killing. 'I said he could have the rest of his money. I think he was suspicious, but he came. He said he didn't want anything more to do with it—claimed he hadn't realized that there was to be a murder involved. He was going to tell you about our little arrangement. He still didn't seem to realize that it was I who had killed her. I told you, he wasn't too bright.'

'And you threatened him with your Smith and Wesson?'

Pritchard showed no surprise that they should know the details of his firearm. His apparent acceptance now of their omniscience was making him talk quite freely. 'Yes. I couldn't remember whether there would be anything for him to stand on in that barn, so I took my own stool. I was going to burn it later this afternoon.' He looked at the surface of the stool's seat, at the tell-tale scratches in the blue paint, where Everton Smith's boots had kicked desperately in their last search for a foothold. 'I made him climb on to the stool and put the rope round his neck. He still thought at first that I was just trying to scare him, but he couldn't take his eyes off the mouth of the gun. He was right to be scared, I suppose: I'd have shot him if I'd needed to. But I preferred to make it look like suicide if I could.'

His hand had strayed unconsciously towards the right-hand pocket of his jacket as he spoke. Lambert, acutely vigilant against any sudden move by the man in the chair, reached with deliberate slowness to that pocket and extracted the pistol on which Pritchard's hand had almost come to rest. Pritchard merely nodded as it passed across his vision and into the polythene bag which Hook produced like a conjuror to receive it.

The killer smiled at the remembrance of the boy's naïvety and his own cunning. 'I told him then about how I'd killed Laura; how I'd weighted the body and dumped it in the river within a few yards of where we were. That was the moment when he realized what I planned to do with him. I kicked the stool away then. It was all over very quickly.'

He was like a vet offering consolation to a bereaved pet owner.

There was the sound of a vehicle drawing up outside. The police car brought the first noise for a long time from outside that claustrophobic old room. Pritchard looked up at the superintendent, almost in appeal, as if he wanted this wrapped up before others intruded upon the scene. Lambert said, 'You were always the likeliest source of Smith's sudden wealth. You were the only one who had had much previous contact with him. You were also the only one of our suspects with a firearm licence. That seemed significant once we were sure that Smith hadn't killed himself willingly; he must have been threatened with something to make him climb on to that stool.'

Pritchard offered no resistance as he was led out to the car between the two uniformed men. They took a length of picture cord from him. He looked at it dully in the policeman's hands as they drove away, as if he comprehended for the first time that even a third murder would not have made him safe.

Sue Hendry had been carried through the exchanges by her passionate hatred of the man who had killed her lover. With his departure, she was suddenly near to collapse. Lambert said, 'I'm sorry I had to put you through that. We needed him to talk before he put himself in the hands of a clever lawyer.'

She nodded. 'I want him convicted even more than you do.'

'Why did he come here?'

'I rang him at lunch-time. I thought it must be him from the start, but I couldn't see how he could have done it. I suppose I wanted it to be him, but I wasn't certain until I heard about the gardener boy being killed. Then I thought like you that he was the only one who would have done that. I made the mistake of ringing him up to see what he had to say about Everton Smith's death. He was round here within half an hour.'

Hook said, 'There was no reply when I tried to get through. Presumably he didn't let you answer the phone.'

'No. He made me ring the office to say I couldn't get in. Then, once he had me afraid, he seemed to enjoy playing cat and mouse with me.' Suddenly she was in tears. 'I didn't know about Laura being killed before he left for Spain, but I was sure he'd done it.'

They were therapeutic tears. She insisted she was fit to go into the office now, and rang in to say she was coming. Lambert decided that action would be the best medicine; no good would come of her sitting alone in the room where she had come so near to death. They followed her car slowly down the drive from her cottage and out on to the lane, watching her accelerate slowly back into the busy life that was to be her salvation.

As the old Vauxhall moved steadily over the rolling green landscape towards the CID room at Oldford, Superintendent and Sergeant caught the familiar sight of the Severn snaking below them, blue and tranquil for the most part, silvered on one huge bend by the high June sun. The great river had run this way long before men came to use its waters and stain it with their blood. It would no doubt be here another million years after this latest evil in the human world.

The concerns of man seemed very small against this natural backdrop. And that to Lambert was a sort of consolation.